THE VOICE OF MANUSH

W0082149

The Voice of Manush

A Novel by
Victor Walter

WHITE PINE PRESS • FREDONIA, NEW YORK

Acknowledgments:
I want to honor the memory of Robie Macauley and to thank Mack Faith, Mary Nash, Gladys Swan, and Gordon Weaver, great teachers, good friends.
I am grateful to all the friends who helped, especially Steve Anderson, Karen Baart, C. Darren Butler, David Cooperman, Natasha Walter Fisk, Ruth Ice, Robert Leinbach, Robert Meadow, Michael V. Miller, Holly Mockovak, Susan Phillips, Pamela Schechtmann, Maria Stowe, Jenia Walter, Richard Wolfe, Kurt Wolff, Roslyn Zinn, Howard Zinn, and my amiable editor, Elaine LaMattina.
Some passages of "First Movement" appeared in a story, "Father's Business," *New England Review,* Vol. 13 (1991); part of "Scherzo" was published as "The Merlin's Eye" in *Magic Realism,* Vol. 4 (1993).

Publication of this book was made possible, in part, by grants from the National Endowment for the Arts and the New York State Council on the Arts.

Cover painting: Valerie Walawender

Book Design: Watershed Design

Manufactured in the United States of America.

First printing 1996

10 9 8 7 6 5 4 3 2 1

ISBN 1-877727-60-1

Published by White Pine Press
10 Village Square, Fredonia, New York 14063

For Ruth

Contents

Even today, great music inspires myths. At first, mythologies needed music because the old stories were sung. But music lived before the creation of the world, before the beginning of time. God sang to himself in the void, and the sound of God tolled over the deep.

—Odisseo Saggio
The Folklore of Music

THE VOICE OF MANUSH

PRELUDE

Shiva meditated on a sacred mountain top with his consort Parvati by his side. After a million years of meditation, she was getting bored. She wanted to dance. Shiva was not interested. She pouted. "I can't meditate all the time." Going to Brahma, the Creator, she pleaded, "Make something to amuse me." Brahma created Manush, the first human.

Manush was clever with his hands, but had no voice. While Shiva meditated, Parvati slipped off the mountain top, sang to Manush. She sang the music of heaven and earth, stories of dawn and dusk, wind and water, stars and sun, clouds, storms, mountains. The music filled his heart, and he trembled with excitement.

First he made tools. Then he cut wood and shaped it. With her permission, he cut four of her hairs to serve as strings. Finally he strung a bow with the fibers of vines. He practiced for a hundred years until he could play the music in his heart. When all of Parvati's music flowed out of his heart, his mind created the *csárdás*.

"What's that I hear?" Shiva asked Parvati.

"The voice of Manush," she replied. Shiva leaped off the top of the mountain and began to dance. The world pulsed with the cosmic energy of his movements. Parvati rejoiced, danced with him.

While they danced, the enemy of the gods, Ravana, a demon with twenty arms, fled from his prison under Shiva's mountain. As long as Shiva sat there, Ravana could not escape, even though he shook the world, pounding the rock walls with his twenty fists. Now he burst out of the mountain and ran away. From a distance he watched the gods dancing to the voice of Manush. When night came and the gods rested, Ravana crept up while Manush slept, stole his instrument, ran to the other side of the world. When he learned to play it, he thought, he would have power to control the gods by making them dance.

Manush grieved day and night for his lost instrument. Brahma replaced it with a voice that issued from his throat. Manush learned to speak and cry and sing but felt it was a poor substitute. To comfort him, Brahma created Manushi, the first woman, who also learned to speak and cry and sing. Their children, the first people born on earth, were called *manava*, "descendants of Manush." They were the first Gypsies.

Feverishly, Manush made one instrument after another, but none of them satisfied him. He and his wife and their children started to wander all over the world, looking for the voice of Manush. Disappointed with these restless Gypsies, Brahma changed the design of humans and made a new race, the *gadje*, hoping they would be less trouble.

Meanwhile, on the other side of the world, Ravana tried to play the voice of Manush. Each one of his twenty hands insisted on taking a turn, and every day a different hand would try to master the strings. When its turn came again, each hand had forgotten what it learned nineteen days before. Enraged, Ravana threw the instrument against a granite boulder. It broke into three parts, and he slunk away into the lower world.

Eventually, the *gadje* found the three parts, and from them constructed the violin, the viola, and the cello.

FIRST MOVEMENT: SHADOW VALLEY

To wretched mortals
all forms of death are hateful.
—Homer, Odyssey

1

Music has the last word. After all that happened, I still believe in the triumph of music over death.

I sit on the porch to play my violin, and kids run up the hill to see the old man who repairs fiddles, bakes cookies, tells stories. I love to have them around, but not today. I don't want children here when the Leech comes, not because he'd take them before their time, but because everything in me strains to keep them away from him.

I get intimations now before each visit of his, nothing more than a hunch, a shiver in my chest. That worries me. About a year before he took her, my mother knew in advance every time he showed up.

He'll ride the bus today because he enjoys human transportation, prefers crowds, likes to touch people. He'll mingle and ask directions, ask how to get to Shadow Valley, Vermont.

He'll get off the bus between Montpelier and Waterbury at Riddle Depot, nothing more than a gas station attached to a large convenience store called Winky's. He knows exactly where I am, but he'll ask where to find Marko Manava, just to get a response. People will see a man with a black hat and wrinkled face the color of ashes, a man carrying a black bag and wearing a dark suit on a hot day. They'll notice but forget.

Here at the north end of the Green Mountains, the Mad River sends tributaries down Shadow Valley, streams that form Shadow Pond. He'll walk from the bus stop, five miles down a dirt road to the village at the edge of the pond. Then he'll climb the hill and find me waiting on the porch. It's a perfect summer day, not too hot, with a fresh breeze gathering smells from the fields, the woods, and the pond. This is a big old house. I never actually counted, but I like to think it has seventy doors and windows, like Merlin's house.

The kids who run up the hill to hear my stories and listen to the fiddle are fascinated by my ears. "Please, Marko, please. Wiggle them! Just one more time." These vast ears stick out of my hair like islands on a frothy sea. Little Mamo, my Gypsy foster mother, used to call me *kannengro*, a Romany term for a thing with long ears—a donkey or rabbit. The one thing that stays the same when I change shape is my ears.

In this natural body I'm a tall, gaunt man with dark eyes in a rough brown face with the beak of an eagle and hair down to my shoulders, gray and black hair that fails to cover my ears. I used to be sensitive about them until I heard a jazz musician praise a great performer by saying "that cat's got big ears." I wear dungarees and a short-sleeved denim shirt, the gray hair on my arms curling up like wool, and I pad about in leather moccasins.

Don't think I never get off the porch. In the evening, I often stroll down the hill to the general store, sit by the wood stove with the old folks, tell stories. Tales are green plants of the mind. Without them we die. And don't get the impression I never get out of Shadow Valley or that I never have any fun. During the concert season, I play in a community orchestra and drive into the Boston area every Wednesday to rehearse. The rest of the time I try to live quietly, but anyone who wants a quiet life should not be a Manava.

What a way to spend my golden years. Sitting on this porch, waiting for the Leech.

2

He didn't show up. Yet, I still had this creepy feeling in my chest, and waited for him.

A leech is a repulsive worm that sucks your blood, and it's also an archaic term for a doctor. I got the idea of calling him "Leech" from an old poem by William Morris:

> As one who lays all hope aside,
> Because the leech has said his life must end.

Around sundown I took a phone call from a man who didn't identify himself, but from the accent I guessed he was a Micmac. I was born an Omaha and have no kinship with Micmacs whatsoever, but they like my work and keep me busy. The man on the phone urged me to drive to Boston and heal Jake Two Rivers, who was almost dead.

I followed his instructions. How come? you may wonder. Why rush to the bedside of a man I never heard of before? Because I had this feeling inside, this shiver in my chest, a feeling I can't describe. Eventually, they would pay me for my work, but I don't wrangle with the Leech just for the money.

I drove south on Rt. 91, keeping the needle at the speed limit, breathed deep, reaching for a calm state of mind. On Rt. 2 between Gardner and Leominster, I heard the viola theme from the second movement of Harold in Italy, heard the viola's song in my head, punctuated by church bells—harp and low strings imitating the sound of bells, harp and low strings answered by horns and bassoons. When I reached Memorial Drive in Cambridge, flute, oboe, and harp took over the bells—high bells like chimes—flute, oboe, and harp answered by horns. *March of the Pilgrims.*

I turned down Mass Avenue, rummaged in my pocket for Jake's address in the South End. Right to Franklin Street. Then left to the straggly open field they call Injun Park—ruined benches, broken glass, patches of grass. Left again on Dover Street to a gray three-decker, an old wooden firetrap with most of the paint gone, a Greek column missing from the porch, a broken window in front. No names downstairs, no mailboxes. The hallway stank of urine. On the second floor, I knocked. No answer at that door. I tried another. A man in a clean white shirt, black pants, and tan Panama hat opened the door wide.

"I'm Marko Manava. Did you call me?"

"Not me," the man said.

"I came to take care of Jake Two Rivers."

"He's here all right."

"Marko Manava," I repeated, offering my hand.

"Donald," he said, looking at my hand.

"Is that your family name or your first name?" I asked.

He glared at me suspiciously. "Call me Don." I edged past him into the room. An uncovered, smeared mattress lay under a bare light bulb in the middle of the floor. "They bring him off the street," Don said.

"Are you a relative of his?" I asked.

"Maybe."

"Don't you know?" I asked impatiently.

"My wife's his cousin."

"Then you are related. By marriage."

"She's dead though."

"I'm sorry," I replied.

He shouted in alarm, "I didn't kill her!"

Taken aback, I said, "I didn't say you did."

"I know it!" he growled impatiently. I saw a bedroom without a door, walked around the mattress to look inside. "I give him the bed," Don explained.

"Does he have any kinfolk?" I asked.

He handed me a slip of paper with a number written in pencil. "His son."

"Why isn't his son here?" I asked.

"Because I didn't call him yet," he snapped.

Jake Two Rivers lay on the bed, his feet bare, but dressed in a blue workshirt and dungarees, eyes open, watching me. He coughed. "What you gonna do?" Don asked.

I sat on the bed beside Jake, took his hand, which felt dead. Jake said in a hoarse voice, "Glad you made it."

He coughed, spat blood into a red bandanna, talked about

hard living, his drinking problem, wanting to die with his children around him. He wanted to beg forgiveness for the neglect they suffered when they were young.

Don stood in the doorway of the bedroom and asked, "You just gonna let him die?"

We heard a knock on the door, and as Jake closed his eyes, I said hang on, here comes the doctor. Don took one look and ran away, trampling the mattress on the floor of the front room, clattered down the stairs. Later, when they paid me, I found out why. The Leech took the form of a well-known local doctor, an ancient sawbones who treated whores and junkies, a bald old man with a red face and threadbare suit who carried an old-fashioned doctor's bag. But the doctor had been dead two years. That's why Don fled.

"I expected you all day," I complained to the Leech, and he replied, "Well here I am." He set down his black bag and we faced each other over Jake Two Rivers, who stopped coughing and sank into a coma. Jake's brown face turned the color of ashes.

"Your move," the Leech said.

"I want to keep Jake," I replied. "Long enough for him to see his children."

"Since when do I wait around till you're ready?"

"Look, you took three in a row. It's time I kept one."

"You're crowding me, Marko."

That was just part of the game. He wouldn't let me in the room if he didn't want to play. "Well I'm too old for this kind of work," I said. "Maybe you should take me instead. Then you can stick to your boring schedule. Without me around to interfere, you can go like a route man, pick up a dozen corpses here, two dozen there."

"Wise guy!" he said. "How much time do you want to give him?"

"Two months."

He picked up his bag, turned to the door. "Thirty days, not a minute more."

"Forty-five," I bargained. "You're getting him for eternity. What's a few more days? You won't lose your job over it."

"Who do you think you are?" He sounded annoyed.

"Forty-five." I repeated. "Look, what the hell difference does it make to you? Fifteen lousy days."

His voice softened. "Forty-five days," he agreed.

"Thank you."

With his hand on the knob, he looked back, and said, "Get it straight, Marko. You're working for me."

"That's what you think," I replied as he went out the door. Jake Two Rivers breathed easy and sat up. The color came back to his face. I helped him with his shoes, went downstairs and phoned his son.

Even though I felt very tired, I drove back home with music in my head. Harold in Italy again. *La daa la daa, la daa-dee dum daa-dee la.* The viola theme from *Harold in Italy,* an intense motif—two descending intervals, a rising arpeggio, a falling three-note figure. It pursued me, ever since I played it in Liverpool. Now its haunting presence kept me from dozing at the wheel, and I drove as fast as I dared. I'll be exhausted all day, I thought, but I'm not too old to do this.

3

It's hard to guess my age because I take care of myself, but sometimes I sound as old as Pesh, my foster grandfather would have said. Nobody knows how old Pesh is, but he's prehistoric. Gypsies of the Manava family claim Pesh is still alive because Death won't take him.

I was born in 1910, the year Mark Twain died, and if I don't talk old, who will? I remember what it was like when I was a kid before the first world war and what it felt like to be an Indian. Nobody called us Native Americans in those days. My mother was an Omaha shaman, but when she died I was adopted by Gypsies. My adoptive grandfather was a master luthier, a wizard with string instruments. So that makes me foster grandson of a wizard and biological son of a witch. Now I'm the wizard of Shadow Valley—in the old lost sense. *Wysard.* Wise guy.

I still claim to be an Omaha, part of me does, even though I was raised by Gypsies, but I have no quarrel with being Gypsy and Omaha at the same time. My right hand holds my left hand in peace and friendship.

I've done a lot of things in my time, studied violin in a conservatory, got kicked out of medical school, worked as an electrical engineer. But what am I right now? A healer, a musician, and a luthier.

As a healer, my purpose in the world is to rescue people and beasts from decay. It sets me up for adventures with Death. But life interests me more than Death. I'm a musician and love the viola, even though I haven't felt content with an ordinary viola since I played The Destiny, the instrument Gypsies call Voice of Manush. And I'll always be a luthier, a fiddle maker. Everything I know about the craft I learned from my grandfather. Music comes to me from the inside—from the very seed and structure of sound. And because I'm all these things—healer, musician, violin maker—music is for me a matter of life and death.

When the Gypsies adopted me, Little Mamo said, "Let's make vows. You give us your love, and we give you our ancestors." I didn't know I'd inherit the Manava family obsession—to spend my life chasing the Voice of Manush. So it doesn't matter how many people I seem to be because all of me gets consumed in that single fire.

4

A long time ago in Hungary, a famous Gypsy fiddler named Manava used to go around performing in the inns. He played such sad and moving tunes that everything wept, including the bushes outside and the blades of grass. Even Death, who sat in an old willow tree on the edge of a swamp, was carried away by the melancholy tunes, and disguised as an old man, he approached the Gypsy, asked the reason for such great lamentation. "It's because I'm so poor," the Gypsy explained.

"Oh I can take care of that," Death disguised as an old man replied. "I'll make you rich, but in return, you must give me the thing you love most."

"Well, the thing I love most is this fiddle, but how would I get along without it?"

"You won't need it when you're rich," Death said. "I'll give you more gold than you can spend."

The Gypsy thought about it, and asked, "What will you do with the fiddle?"

"Play it all over. People will follow me anywhere I want to lead them." Then Death revealed his true identity to the Gypsy, who was not a bit scared, but smiled to himself.

They flew through the air to a waterfall between mountains, and Death dug into a shallow part of the stream, bringing up a handful of gold nuggets. "The riverbed and the cave behind the waterfall are full of gold," Death said. "It's all yours, but give me your fiddle."

The Gypsy examined the gold and replied, "You kept your word, and now I'll keep my part of the bargain. But permit me to say a last farewell to my fiddle."

The Gypsy played with such intense feeling that not only Death but everything on earth wept, and heaven as well. As the last note trailed away, the Gypsy placed his lips on the face of the violin. Kissing the fiddle, he also sucked the air out of the soundholes before he handed it to Death, who vanished as neatly as the mist disappears before the rising sun. The Gypsy laughed, sat down, filled his clay pipe, and had a smoke before he started picking up gold.

Three days later, the Gypsy was rich, but he yearned for his fiddle. Sitting on a pile of gold, he asked, "Death, what takes you so long? You're a clever fellow, but I'm not exactly stupid."

Suddenly, Death appeared before him in a rage. "Take back your damn fiddle! It doesn't work for me, and I made a bad bargain. You have the gold, but I can't attract people with the sound of your violin. Why don't I play like you?"

Taking the fiddle out of Death's hand, the Gypsy explained, "It's not your fault. I gave you the fiddle, according to our bargain, but I kept the soul for myself." He placed his lips to a soundhole, breathed into it, tucked the fiddle under his chin, and played such a fiery *csárdás* that Death wiggled and skipped about, unable to keep from dancing.

When he finished, Death said, "What a fool I am to get cheated by a Gypsy. Well, what's done is done. You have the gold as well as the fiddle. Nevertheless, I'm not as big a fool as you think. Your playing is so sad, it will entice men and women and children into my clutches."

That's what you think, the Gypsy thought.

Since that day, the gold is spent and the Gypsy is poor again, but he receives money for playing the *csárdás*, which nobody else can play with the same effect, and he plays it all over the world. He still performs melancholy tunes that make people cry, but he also plays music to make them dance. When Death comes for them, he has to wait because they're busy dancing. They all jump and jiggle when the Gypsy performs. Except for Death, who hates to dance.

5

If an instrument doesn't make you dance and sing and cry—
if it doesn't lead out the soul—it's a failure. That's why Gypsies
were made. We're leaders—that's our secret mission, but only
the gods know. The *gadje* think we're merely survivors. The
Creator made us to lead, made us to lead out the souls of men
and women. Some of us play with tarot cards. Others tell tales
of enchantment. The rest of us make music.

These days luthier and virtuoso are separate persons, but
when you put them together they're like gods. Together the
luthier and the artist create a personality—the living voice.
Every instrument is alive. The first man on earth was a Gypsy
and the Creator made him both a luthier and a virtuoso, made
him like one of the gods. He played music that made Shiva
dance, the primal dance that set the world in motion. Shiva
danced to the Voice of Manush.

That's the story my ancestor, Manava Mihaly, told Stradivari. They were good friends. Stradivari acquired his best wood, water cured and treated, from the Gypsy. Mihaly would leave boards submerged in nets in different streams. Hatcheries of fiddles. He'd leave them by a waterfall to absorb the energy of the stream. He said if you took two boards from the same tree but cured one in the Tiber and the other in the Ticino, they came out singing different sounds. Different nymphs made different fiddles. Stradivari believed him and, hearing the same thing, selected his boards with an ear to the nymphs.

He regarded the Gypsy as a master luthier, a peer, and when Mihaly visited Stradivari, he worked on his own instruments, right along with Francesco and Omobono, Stradivari's sons. Mihaly followed their acoustic experiments with great interest. In return, he revealed old secrets of Gypsy violin making, which Stradivari tested. Mihaly told Stradivari he wanted a copy of the world's first musical instrument, the voice of the first man.

He wanted it for religious reasons. Imagine a Jewish or Christian family named Adams, a pious family who told the biblical story of Creation and the Garden of Eden over and over. They would feel a special relation to Adam. In the tradition of the Manava family, who wandered out of India a long time ago, Manush was the first man.

Mihaly wanted Stradivari to reconstruct the voice of Manush. In return, he promised the Gypsies would supply Stradivari and his sons with the finest boards of spruce and maple as long as they should live. Intrigued by the challenge, Stradivari set to work and produced the instrument with three voices.

6

I slept late after the long drive home from Boston, and the phone woke me. A man with a thick accent said, "I want to address Manava Marko." Gypsies don't write letters, but oh how they use the telephone!

"Speaking," I mumbled, lying on my back, the phone against my ear. "Who are you?"

"Manava Lashi. In Athens I am calling." That nudged me wide awake, cleared my head. Lashi Manava was one of the most distinguished names in Gypsy music, a virtuoso on flute, sylvan pipes, syrinx, and a composer who transformed the Pan flute into a concert instrument. Born in Budapest, he performed all over, made recordings, wrote beautiful music. I had heard he was living in Greece now. "Do you know who I am?" he asked.

"*Ratniken chiriclo*," I answered, which means the nightingale.

He laughed with a high giggle, then caught his breath and inquired, "*Sar shin sarla, meero rye*," How are you this evening, sir?

It was still morning in Vermont. "*Koshti sarla*," Good evening, I replied. "*Sore simensar si men*," You and I are relatives, be informal. We continued the conversation in Romany. "To what do I owe this honor of hearing your voice?"

"Holy business, brother. Manava business." He tested me with the family riddle. "What's the name of the only thing on earth that has one body and three voices?"

"MONush!" I replied. That's the correct pronunciation, MONush. The way Gypsies say it. In Romany, Manush means man or human, very close to the Sanskrit word, *manasha*, which means the same thing. The riddle has two meanings. A human has one voice in childhood, another as an adult, and a third voice in old age. But that's only the surface meaning. The deeper one is the name of the mysterious instrument Paganini renamed The Destiny.

"You know what happened in Istanbul?" Lashi asked.

"I know no more than a child."

"Tornapo died in prison."

"Yes. Who's the new *voivode*?"

"Wentzelo, and he's got deep ideas for the new regime."

"How did the others fare in prison?"

"*Boccale pers*," Hungry bellies. "And they came down with the stinking sickness. The Turks killed Tornapo."

"Murdered him?"

"Filthy Turkish prison. Same thing."

"*Si covar*. Tell me Wentzelo's plans."

"He wants to recover the Voice and proclaim a Glory Year.

That's why I telephoned you."

"Why me?"

"Because, dear brother, we understand you played it."

I swallowed, tried to sound nonchalant. "Whatever gave you that idea?"

"Family gossip. *Avata acoi!* Come thou here! Join the search."

"The Voice is in exile."

"*Padlo pawni,*" Across the water. Shifting to English, he added, "According to the superstition..." He wanted me to understand he didn't necessarily believe all that stuff.

Unwilling to hear condescending remarks about Gypsy legend, I interrupted, "I know, I know."

"Brother Marko, one thing I don't understand. You're a Manava, and the Voice was in your hands. Why didn't it steal you?"

"Probably not ready to come home. Family travelled empty when Tornapo was *voivode*. He didn't want the responsibility of keeping the Voice. That's why it stayed in Liverpool."

Lashi sighed. "Things are different now. I'm glad you'll cooperate."

"I'm an old man," I protested.

"*Tatcho.* But what's old got to do with it?"

"I was hoping for a quiet year."

He giggled. "Anyone who wants a quiet life should not be a Manava."

"I'll do what I can."

"*Paracro tute,*" I thank you. "*Ja Develhi!*" Go with God!

"It was an honor to speak with you," I said.

"*Aukko to pios adrey Romanes,*" We drink to your health in

38

Romany, he concluded.

"*Bahtalo drom!*" Lucky road! I replied, and hung up the phone.

I thought about it all day. If the world hears a Manava play the Voice of Manush, the family is rewarded by a Glory Year, a year in which nobody in the family dies. It also means no woman of our blood is barren or miscarries. And twelve months of no misfortune on the road, no sickness in our midst, nobody in prison or hospital. A Glory Year for the Manava family is followed by another year of pretty good luck for Gypsies all over the world.

As far as I knew, the Manavas had no Glory Year in this century. What if, what if? Even if I didn't believe the legend, what if I were to recover the Voice and play it in concert? Gypsies all over the world would hear about it. Wouldn't it be a blessing? Magic or no magic—it would boost morale, help us thrive. No great good thing has happened to Gypsies since the years of catastrophe, since Hitler tried to wipe us out.

The idea set fire to my imagination. What if I found the lost trio Mozart wrote for the Voice—and played it? And on a larger scale, how about a symphony? What if I played the work Berlioz originally wrote for it, the music Paganini commissioned for the Voice—*Harold in Italy?* A hundred instruments singing along with the Voice! What a concert! It would be my finest moment, to play the Voice to the world, to give my people a Glory Year.

But I calmed down and felt reluctant. According to the legend, when the family was ready, the Voice found its way back. They didn't need me. Besides, I was in Vermont, not out on the *puszta* or in Liverpool. And I had done enough!

7

My first inkling of The Destiny came when I was a boy in Brooklyn, seated one day at my bench in the workshop of my grandfather, Papio Tamás. I was working on a project for Mr. Jacobson's science class at David A. Boody Junior High School. Papio Tamás was repairing a viola on the long table by the window. Suddenly he screamed and flapped his elbows up and down. "Quack-quack! Quack-quack!" he shouted, and pushed the instrument away from him. He turned to me and said, "I'm a luthier, but they want a magician. They expect me to make a nightingale out of a duck."

He picked up the viola, carried it over to my bench so I could look at it. Once again he squinted through the f-holes at the ticket. "What criminal made this stupid thing? Proportions all wrong." Then he turned to me. "The owner brought this hopeless creature all the way from Kansas City. He should have taken it to a veterinarian. This thing belongs in a barnyard, not in an orchestra." Then he paused to inspect what I was doing at the bench. "Experiments," he said. He thrust out the viola in his hand and exclaimed, "This is an experiment that failed!"

He returned to the long table muttering, "Quack-quack!" Thrusting the viola in a rack, he turned to a new violin he was making and worked in silence. About a half hour later he said, "They want magicians." Smoothing the purfling of the unvarnished instrument, he held it up to the light and smiled, "But sometimes we're like gods." He turned it over on its belly, prepared to rub the wood. "Today fiddle makers use sandpaper. No wonder they turn out ducks."

He looked at me with the deepest sorrow and said, "Some day you'll be tempted to use sandpaper." I shook my head vigorously, denying I would ever sink so low. "Sandpaper raises fibers on the surface of the wood," he explained, "leaves it fuzzy. Those hairy little buggers are invisible to the naked eye." He shook his finger at me. "They clog the grain." He held a scraper in front of my eyes, a thin metal blade burnished to a fine edge. "A scraper leaves the wood clean."

In the final stages, Papio Tamás used a scraper made from the blade of a saber. The hard steel edge never got jagged, therefore cut less deeply, never tearing the delicate cornea of the wood. This particular scraper was passed on by his teacher and godfather, Minugia, a great violin maker, the last of the old Cremonese luthiers. Minugia, who died thirty-seven years before I was born, was a living presence in our workshop.

Then for the final smoothing, Papio Tamás used an abrasive grass called horsetail, as well as the skin of the dogfish.

Stradivari gathered the horsetail grass from the muddy banks of rivers and canals in Cremona. Papio Tamás gathered his in Brooklyn. "There are plenty of horse's asses in the world," he told me as we searched for the grasses together, "but they don't grow tails like this."

For the dogfish, he sought out men who fished on Sheepshead Bay. Dogfish are sandsharks, and when they get on the hook, fishermen curse and kill them, throw the little sharks away. But these men saved the fish for Papio Tamás. They liked him and refused to take money. You can't beat the scales of a sandshark when it comes to smoothing wood. He would nail the skins on a board to stretch. Some of them were four feet long. Then he soaked them in fresh water along with the horsetails. After they dried out in cotton wraps, he put them away on a shelf until they were needed.

As he rubbed the new fiddle with abrasive cloth, he looked at me from the corner of his eye, working the cloth over the surface of the violin with quick, decisive strokes. "Luthiers have a great teacher. We study the work of the master." He blew the dust off the violin. "Not a sacred text. Not the book of nature. We study the Book of Stradivari." He laid down the violin and examined some new pegs, rubbing them with horsetails. "Not a book with words in it. Every instrument he made is a lesson, a chapter in the great book. Over a thousand lessons he gave the world, and many perished or remained unknown. But there are still more than six hundred for us to study. That's why I go to Mecca."

I knew what he meant. Every few years, Papio Tamás would clean up the shop, put everything in order, and say, "I'm getting ready for the pilgrimage." Then he traveled to Europe, visiting old friends and relatives, but in Italy he'd go straight to Cremona and spend a week or so of intense devotion in whatever place held the Stradivari relics. I say devotion because he already knew by heart the appearance and measurements of every mold, form, piece of wood, and every tool in the collection. All the luthiers in the city knew him, looked forward to his visits. They would talk shop, gossip about good and bad instruments, remember the old days. "We, the disciples," he continued, "never stop learning. Our hands tremble, we stumble, we see through a glass darkly. Each fiddle we make is an experiment."

I listened intently but kept working at my bench. Watching me take measurements, he added, "Some day I'll tell you about Stradivari's great experiment. He made an instrument for Manava Mihaly, maybe three or four great-uncles ago. I learned about it in Paris, heard the story in the workshop of Vuillaume, from the lips of Minugia, who was close to Paganini—like a second son. Instead of making a violin or viola or cello, Stradivari ventured into the unknown. He created The Destiny."

8

I played with the tools on my grandfather's bench, kept asking questions. He watched me tinker with bits of wood and violin strings. "You will help me in the shop," Papio Tamás announced, appointing me by this simple declaration as his apprentice. I learned to make simple repairs.

"You hear a lot of nonsense about this craft," he explained. "Making music is an art, but to make an instrument requires science. Everything depends on precise measurement and the iron laws of acoustics. The harmonic series you must obey. If you break the law, you're out of luck. The world is full of criminal violin makers, but they ought to be banished from the trade. Gypsy rubbish is the worst. They try to hoodwink the public with their secret lore. They bury a new violin in a sacred place at the full moon with incantations. Bury it sewed up in a cow's bladder filled with horseshit. To cook it, they say.

You know what that is?"

I shrugged to declare my innocence.

"It's horseshit, that's what it is. Just plain horseshit."

I loved the smells of wood and glue. When I swept the floor, I leaned over to pick up curly shavings, ran them through my fingers, held them under my nose. I keep that big sunlit room inside me, see boards of maple and spruce leaning against the wall, the band saw in the middle, a lathe, grinders, whetstones, and racks full of chisels, knives, and gouges. I see bows hanging on the wall, about a dozen violins waiting in different racks, three or four violas, a cello or two resting in the corner, shelves holding planes of different sizes, jars, pots of glue, jugs of varnish, his workbench by the large front window, a cloth string dangling assorted bridges of violins, violas and cellos looped across another window. I see Papio Tamás seated on a stool in the middle of the room with a maple violin back clasped between his knees and a small plane in his hands, shaving down the liners of a new instrument.

I loved to watch him carve. He entered the wood with precision and respect but with sensual strokes. When he worked on a project that excited him, he wore a white wool cap and a white leather apron, following the example, he said, of his spiritual master, Stradivari.

For Papio Tamás, Antonio Stradivari and Niccolo Paganini were the greatest men who ever lived. He knew all about them from his teacher and godfather, Minugia. Stradivari was in the grave forty-five years when Paganini was born, but in the imagination of Papio Tamás they were intimate friends. He invented conversations between them, never tired of repeating old legends and making up new stories about their relationship.

He gave me several different names. Sometimes he would call me Francesco, after the son of Antonio Stradivari. Then he would call me Paganini. He would play with me, incorporate me into his fantasies. He shaped me by his daydreams, just as he molded a violin to fit the design in his mind. Whatever I was in the shop at any moment was his dream of me.

The shop was my only playground. My favorite game was Indian Revenge. Living in New York made me more belligerent, and I abandoned the peaceful strategy of the Omahas, who never declared war on the United States. He would act out the part of the bluecoats and settlers, and I would be a great chief who masterminded a federation of all the victimized tribes, leading them to victory, driving the whites off the land. Sometimes I made him play the part of Colonel Custer, and in the course of a year he carved me a whole troop of wooden cavalrymen in painted blue uniforms, seated on army mounts, as well as a war party of noble Indians on gorgeous ponies. The figures were ten inches high, and we arranged them in formations on the shop floor. He inspired me to turn out those little statues on my own, and I stayed busy with the lathe and chisels. Later I learned his motive was to teach me to carve.

He said to me, "You know, Chief Hungry Buffalo, I'm only an old Gypsy who never went to university, but I've read the same books they read in school. I'll give you a lesson you can't find in the books—a lesson in Gypsy politics. I have a secret weapon to conquer the white man." He picked up a fiddle, began to play. "Here it is. You make them dance. And when they're dancing, they can't fight."

He would review old wars on the shop floor, discuss international politics, gave me lessons on the Franco-Prussian War, which he remembered vividly, lived through it in Paris soon after he left his father's workshop in Hungary to become what he called a freak of nature: a sedentary Gypsy. As a young luthier in the great workshop of Jean Baptiste Vuillaume, the war made a deep impression on him. For years afterward, he read its history, studied the campaigns.

Papio Tamás arranged eight molds on the floor. "Here are the generals," he said. A cello mold: "There's a fat one." A violin mold: "And a skinny one." On the Prussian side, "Moltke, Manteuffel, Werder, and von Alvensleben. And here are the French generals: MacMahon, Clinchant, Crémer, and Billot. Now we'll put them in the Hall of Mirrors at Versailles and surround them with musicians. Listen to the opening barrage— not cannon but kettle drums. The brass sound a fanfare. The generals are listening. The oboe speaks and they strain with attention. Here come the violins. They're beginning to move their feet. They're dancing. The French and the Germans are in one another's arms. The war is over." Papio Tamás and I sat on the floor, getting wood shavings all over our clothes, me laughing till I got hiccups.

In more serious games, he played Antonio Stradivari. "Francesco," he said, "I'm ninety-three years old, and my time has come. You must carry on. A star will rise in the East. Unto us a child is born. Take your two brothers, Paolo and Omobono. Find the babe. Bring gifts to the holy child. A violin, a viola, a cello. Unto us a genius is given. They shall call his name Paganini."

9

Papio Tamás used to think Stradivari counted The Destiny as an ordinary viola. According to his reckoning, Stradivari made twelve violas and only eleven were accounted for. He thought the missing viola was The Destiny. But now we can identify nineteen Stradivari violas. Still, that's not many, considering he made over eleven hundred instruments in a lifetime of ninety-three years. The usual explanation is there was hardly any demand for violas in those days. But Minugia's old friend, Tarisio, claimed Stradivari made several instruments that were *cosidette viole*—so-called violas.

Perhaps Stradivari never counted them as regular instruments. He made them to carry out acoustic experiments. Internally, they were not conventional, even though he stuck to the external shape and size of the viola. When he found out what he wanted to know, he destroyed them or gave away parts to the Gypsies. All except one. Tarisio said it was commissioned by a Gypsy, Manava Mihaly. The Manava family owned it.

It looks like a viola, and when you play in the middle range, it sounds like one. When you play above that, you hear a violin. In the lower register, it sounds like a cello. It was the last instrument Stradivari made. When he finished The Destiny, he died. That's what my grandfather heard in Paris. But who knows? They may have been playing with a figure of speech. When the French say, *Il a fini sa destinée,* they mean "He's dead."

Three instruments in one. A miracle. Stradivari achieved the impossible. He squared the circle.

Paganini wanted it. He could handle any instrument of any size. Envious people said it was because he was such a showoff. Tarisio knew better. The Destiny was a miracle that demanded a magician. A miracle of living sound. How could Paganini keep his hands off it?

10

La daa la daa, la daa-dee dum daa-dee la.
Unmistakable. Unforgettable. Technically speaking, *Harold in Italy* is not the greatest viola solo, but I have always loved it. I remembered the first time I played it in the high school orchestra. The Berlioz symphony opened with a brooding introduction, English horn against the winds, violas and celli dark against the violins. I stood alone in the shadow, a romantic outsider, stood in silence to dramatize my isolation from the orchestra, until the thirty-eighth measure, when I sounded the Harold theme, a simple, passionate, haunting idea. The melody on the solo viola was a contemplative presence haunting all four movements, its character unchanged by swirling events. Harold *was* the viola.

I had always loved the melody, but the haunting started after I played it on The Destiny. When I didn't expect it, the music entered my head, sometimes while I was driving, or falling asleep, or even when I played an ordinary viola. Just before I touched the strings, sometimes, I heard the motif from Harold, impeccably performed, and with the unmistakable timbre and sonority of music played on The Destiny. It didn't drive me crazy, as an ordinary tune did when I could not get it out of my head. It gave me comfort.

Great music brings me to the threshold of understanding. But the work of Mozart, Bach, Beethoven—even Berlioz—performed on The Destiny, takes me over the threshold. When I hear it, I know something important, even though I can't express in words what I learned. The haunting started after I went to Liverpool to document a fake name.

We all start with names given to satisfy others—to please our parents, to represent their dreams. But to reach fulfillment, we need many names. Russell Flambard faked my documents. For a trusted old customer like me, he would take on any job— except to counterfeit money, his one scruple. Too risky, he thought. He was a master forger who elevated simulation to a fine art. The world's grand master of sham.

To all appearances, Russell had a respectable business. He worked in a converted warehouse with a small crew, restoring old paintings. A hidden door in the basement wall led into a large, well-lit converted bomb shelter, which looked like a printer's shop, where a larger crew—four men and two women, all in rubber aprons—helped him carry on his real work: the business of deception.

Russell looked like a walrus imitating an Edwardian gentleman. He liked to wear a bowler, which sat over a round face with great jowls, long mustaches, rimless spectacles. A few years ago, he greeted me warmly, and I said he looked elegant. He wore a high collar, tweed lounge suit, fancy waistcoat. Patting his belly, he replied, "Actually, I prefer a more gaudy tweed, but gentlemen with abdominal convexity should use discretion."

He took me to lunch at a chip shop some distance away from his establishment. "I need the real thing," he said. "Nothing disgusts me more than bogus fish and chips. The new Asian shops are forcing authentic chippers out of business. Damned immigration is changing the character of British nourishment."

After lunch he took me on a tour of his factory. "I should take on more crew, but it's hard to find people I can trust," he said. "The facsimilation industry is booming. We still do a lot of bread and butter work—passports, fake bills of sale, licenses of all sorts, bills of lading, commercial documents, certificates. But as you know I'm at heart an artist. I like to work for people with imagination."

In one corner, a woman leaned over a canvas laid flat on a table, working in oils and referring to several color photographs. "We always have an old master going. Oil sheikhs gobble them up. This portrait from the school of Roger van der Weyden will eventually go to a rich man in Abu Dhabi who thinks he collects Flemish paintings. Over here is the Bible belt," he said, pointing to a wide bench. "Coverdale Bibles keep us in fish and chips; we've even done a Gutenberg." From another bench he called out, "Manuscripts. We're very busy with orders from Texas. University libraries there are hungry for medieval manuscripts, and a couple of dealers, who are regular customers now, find it less risky to sell one of our forgeries than to pinch an original from some place like Yale.

"I travel a lot for the right materials. For paintings, I go to Spain and southern France to find pigments. But my true love is paper. To match old paper, I'll sail the seven seas. I searched Egypt and Cypress to find correct rag linen. Watermarks are my pride and joy. No one can challenge my watermarks."

I counted out money to pay Russell for fake passports he had turned out for me, but when I slid the wallet back into my pocket, he touched my arm lightly and said with a smile, "And there's V.A.T." I stood there puzzled. In conventional retailing, Value Added Tax was a British surcharge on the selling price. Was my old friend holding me up for a bit more cash? His grin expanded, and he explained, "It means Violist Asking for a Teacher."

He led me to one of the benches where a young woman was sewing the binding of a leather volume. She was in her late twenties, I guessed, and she smiled nervously, with nice straight teeth in a round, pretty face. "This is Kate Spaulding," he said. She shook hands. "He agreed to give you a lesson, Kate," Russell lied.

We left the workshop, and the three of us stopped at the Laughing Billygoat, near Russell's house, for pints of ale. He handed the pub owner a set of keys. "Throw away the old ones. We installed new locks." The owner looked amused, and Russell turned to me. "He keeps an extra set for us. Kate or me's always leaving them behind in the shop."

"He's being kind," Kate said. "It's usually me."

Russell and Kate lived in a modest two-storey house with beige stucco walls and a tidy garden in front. We went upstairs to a room empty except for an unused fireplace and a few chairs. He brought in two music stands, fished a key out of a blue vase on the mantelpiece, unlocked a mahogany cupboard, brought out an instrument in a black leather case with silver trimming.

"This is a nice viola," he said. "Kate wants to hear you play it. We got it from a Gypsy who fixes up instruments and tries to palm them off as old masters. This one's a fake Stradivarius. You might enjoy it." He handed it to me, and Kate went out of the room to bring in another viola for herself.

Gypsy boldness interests me, and I found the idea of some crazy trader pretending to sell a Stradivari very stimulating. When I was a boy, dealers were always asking Papio Tamás to look at old instruments they had taken in or to advise them about prospective transactions that made them nervous. This one had a rich orange-amber color and a high ridge around the edge. I squinted at the sound holes and found the label, which showed a little Latin cross between the initials A S enclosed in a triple ring. To the left of the initials, under the left sound hole, the ticket read:

Antonius Stradiuarius Cremonensis
Faciebat Anno 17

The dirt inside reminded me that Gypsies liked to shake ashes from the fireplace and dust from the floor into the instrument to make wood and label appear old. I inspected the back, fashioned from a single piece of maple, observed the manner in which the purfling was inserted into the edges, looked at the carving of the f-holes and the scroll. It was an especially long viola. I pulled out my tape and measured forty-five centimeters. No wonder Kate was asking for help. I smiled at her and said, "For this instrument you don't need a teacher. You need a wrestling coach."

Papio Tamás used to praise my long arms and big hands. "Look at this kid," he would say. "He's built like Paganini."

But the large viola felt almost as light as a violin. I started to play and as the feeling snuck up on me, began to laugh. I laughed so hard, tears came to my eyes. Papio Tamás had taught me all the Gypsy tricks of disguising instruments as antiques, but this one was an authentic Stradivari. The sweetest viola I had ever played, and unusually responsive. Sound leaped from the strings. It seemed to play itself.

Tears in my eyes, I looked at Russell with admiration and gratitude. And just played. The bow danced in my hand, and the instrument began to sing inescapable passages Kate and I were waiting to hear—passages every violist who masters the repertoire must play: the sublime first movement from Berlioz, *Harold in Italy*. But I stopped abruptly. Would they suspect? Had I given it away? Did the pure, soaring voice tell them this instrument was more than a viola?

The upper register sounded like a Stradivari violin. And when I tested the lower register, it had the sonority of a cello. The stories Papio Tamás told me about Stradivari's last masterpiece crept into my mind. I tapped the wood, tasted the varnish. My hands were trembling.

Where did Russell get this instrument, I wondered? I would have gone to England just to play it, even with no other reason to be there. Did he steal it himself? Not likely. Did he commission its theft, or buy it from a thief? Was he fencing string instruments? Or did he really believe it was fake? I sensed the erotic connection between Russell and Kate, guessed this priceless instrument was his gift to her. "Not bad for a Gypsy imitation," I said to him.

The potence of life burned my fingertips. Afraid I had revealed the Manava secret, I tried to play out of tune, just to deceive them, but the instrument refused to make an ugly sound. With great effort, I scratched out a few raspy noises. "This thing has some fatal flaws," I lied. Russell chuckled and left the room, but Kate stared at me as if she were struck with awe. Had she heard the voice within the Voice, the lifesong?

Russell left the two of us alone. "This instrument is an interesting curiosity," I said. "A hybrid experiment cooked up by some Gypsy fiddlemaker. No wonder you found it awkward." I settled it under my chin, lifted the bow, raised my eyebrows. "Let's play," I said.

Kate played well on the other viola, easily at the standard of a talented conservatory student. I wagered to myself she was a dropout from the Royal College of Music. She remained shy, uttered scarcely a word. What had Russell told her about me to inspire such deferential awe? I tried to read her face. She knew she heard something extraordinary when I played the Voice, but I hoped she would attribute it to my virtuosity. She played together with me, following instructions whenever I had something to say. I wondered how she and Russell got along in bed.

Since we were in England, I started with William Walton's concerto. It was a patriotic gesture, like saluting the flag or singing *God Save the Queen*. We played a few duets, then read from Kate's collection of viola music, working on Hindemith's

Swanherder, a passionate, classical statement by a composer who was also a great violist. And of course we concluded by wandering in a lyric glow with Harold in the mountains. But as I played and hummed this ultimate work, Kate put down her instrument and simply listened, her hands in her lap. Was it me she admired or the Voice? Her lips trembled and her lovely eyes grew large as the music carried me away.

When we finished playing and sat in silence, Russell came back into the room. I watched Kate pack the Voice into the black case with silver trimming and hand it to Russell. He placed it in the mahogany cupboard, and I watched him drop the cupboard key into the blue vase on the mantelpiece.

As if some invisible blanket spread over my excitement, I put the questions aside. If I believed it were indeed the legendary viola, then I must heed the legend, which prophesied the Voice always found its own way back to the Manava family. But the rational part of my mind would not let up. Could it be true? That I actually played on The Destiny? Something began for me that day in Liverpool.

The three of us ate dinner together the same night. I felt unexpected sorrow to say farewell.

11

But the Voice would not leave me alone. Music stayed in my ears, clear, perfect, relentless, along with whispers. What more do you want? A gift certificate? You're a Manava. Through you, legend comes true. The Voice will steal you. The Voice is in your hands. Don't leave without it.

I rented a car at the airport, stayed in a hotel overnight, spent hours in deep concentration, reviewing everything I knew about metamorphosis, practiced before a mirror. Down to the last detail, I changed my shape to look like Russell Flambard—bowler hat, rimless glasses, walrus mustache, big belly, fancy waistcoat, tweed suit. Except for the ears. The one thing I cannot change is my ears, but I hoped no one would notice.

Middle of next afternoon, when I was sure Russell and Kate were at work, I checked out of the hotel, drove to their house, parked in front, and in the shape of Russell Flambard, walked into the Laughing Billygoat, slapped the bar and complained in Russell's voice, "Forgot me bloody key."

The owner smiled, wiped his hands on his apron, fished the keys out of a box, slapped the bar in reply, and said, "I hope Kate is laughing, Russell."

No sign of neighbors near Russell's house. I shook my head in wonder. Me burglarizing my old friend's home! Where would this Manava madness lead? I ran upstairs to the room where Kate and I had played, found the key in the blue vase, held my breath as I opened the mahogany cabinet. There it was, the black viola case with silver trimming. Locking the cupboard, I dropped the key in the vase, ran downstairs with the case under my arm, locked the door, deposited the viola in the trunk of the car, hurried back to the pub to return the house key. "Much obliged," I said.

"Pleasure," the owner replied. "Pint of lager, Russell?"

"Later," I shouted from the door. I drove to the airport, turned in the car, waited for my flight to London.

The viola case stayed on my lap. Not until we were airborne did I open it slowly, first one clasp, then the other, peering inside, lifting the instrument out of the case. What I saw made my heart recoil as if I were in mortal danger. In my hands I held an ordinary viola. Not the Voice of Manush. I looked in the soundhole for the ticket. Copy of a Tecchler viola, made in Berlin, 1931.

I felt defeated and frightened. Either Russell or Kate or some unknown hand switched instruments, removed the Voice, put this modest viola in its place. But it also meant The Destiny evaded me. The Voice was not ready to come home.

12

That seemed like a long time ago. Now, out on the porch, I glanced at the sky. Tuesday, July 15, St. Swithin's Day, and not a cloud in sight. I recited to myself:

> St. Swithin's day if thou dost rain
> For forty days it will remain.
> St. Swithin's day if thou be fair
> For forty days 'twill rain na mair.

In the garden, I picked raspberries for a second breakfast, moved to the kitchen, where I mixed some dried cooked grain with berries and nettles, set out a bowl, pitcher of milk, pot of honey. I include nettles in every meal. You'll never get hardening of the arteries if you have nettles in your diet. I like to serve dandelions as well, root and leaf. A weed to the ignorant, but a magic herb to the Gypsy. I lingered over coffee, felt peaceful, wanted to sit on the porch and reflect, enjoy the summer.

Paths were trod for me by the shamans in my mother's family and by my Gypsy ancestors, but where's the freedom in those old tracks? I ask you, where is it? I chose a roving life instead, wandering from one path to another as the spirit moved me, searching my weird. In Old English, *weird* means *fate*. Destiny is fixed, but weird bends and turns, the feature of destiny that's pronounced or expressed.

I should have waited another day to make up my mind. The wizards of Glastonbury warn not to make an important decision on St. Swithin's Day or you'll wind up in a terrible place. That's because St. Swithin asked to be buried away from sacred ground in a vile and nasty grave.

But the next day, the sky grew dark and it rained. So much for St. Swithin's Day prophesies. By evening I sat watching a steady downpour. A solid black sky shut out the moon. Nice rain. I listened to it hiss in the fields, tap the leaves near the house, drip from the gutters. The night felt cool and fresh, the scent of pond hanging in the air. Instead of getting dinner, I sat on the porch thinking. Why did fate choose me for this kind of life? The answer to that one, Gypsies say, is in a song I never heard.

Little Mamo told me, "You give us your love, and we give you our ancestors." There's no me without them. But am I the end of the line? I have only one child, who lives on a Greek island, a child I may never see again.

SCHERZO:
PLAYING WITH DEATH

Our life is a bird
which flies by night,
enters the lighted hall by one door
and swiftly passes out the other.
So come we
who knows whence?
So pass we
who knows whither?
From darkness we come,
to darkness we go.
Our brief illumination
makes not the mystery plain.

—Adapted from Bede,
Ecclesiastical History

*Some Birds
see a lot more than others.*

—Marko Manava

1

Soon after Tamás, my foster grandfather, left Vuillaume's
workshop in Paris to live in America, Misha Sklar, concertmas-
ter of the New York Symphony, introduced him to the luthiers
of Fourth Avenue, and he went to work for Friedrich Brothers
on 26th Street. After a few years, he left them to go into part-
nership with the eccentric Hans Tietgen, who claimed to have
rediscovered the varnish of Cremona. They quarreled all the
time, and Tamás left to start his own business in Little
Hungary before he moved to the place in Brooklyn. He married a Magyar singer, and they had a daughter, but his wife
died of tuberculosis when the child was still young. He never
remarried, and raised Sylvia alone. She grew up to be Little
Mamo, my foster mother.

String players sought him out, schemed to have him work
on their instruments, and by the time the New York Symphony

merged with the Philharmonic, Tamás was the orchestra's most cherished luthier. With more work than he could handle, he refused to hire assistants. "No patience with coffin makers," he explained. Twenty years after Tamás came to America, Josef Kovařík, Dvořák's assistant, discovered him.

Now Kovařík played viola in the New York Philharmonic for many years, but that was long after Dvořák's time in America. In 1892, when the composer was Director of the National Conservatory, young Kovařík lived in the Dvořák household, worked on the faculty of the conservatory, became the faithful shadow of the maestro. My grandfather repaired Kovařík's instruments, and one day the young man brought Dvořák to his shop because the maestro was interested in Gypsies. Dvořák stayed all afternoon, watching Tamás scrape. He leaned over the bench, thrust his whiskers, which stuck out like wires, into the work. The composer said he believed American Indians and Gypsies might have descended from the same stock. Perhaps there was an historic connection between Indian and Gypsy music. "Listen to the syncopation!" he urged.

"With all due respect to you maestro, it's a crazy idea," Tamás replied. The conversation intrigued Dvořák, and after that, Tamás often walked with them on Sundays, from the Dvořák house on 17th Street up to Central Park to listen to the birds, or out to the railway station to hear the locomotives. Dvořák liked to have Tamás around to talk him out of his crazy idea.

In the following year, Kovařík persuaded Dvořák to spend summer vacation in his hometown, Spillville, Iowa, where the maestro would feel at home. A good place to compose, away from the city, and a Bohemian community where he could hear Czech on the street, go to a Czech church. He could celebrate his fifty-second birthday in a place that would remind him of Bohemia.

Dvořák warmed to the plan. He was here to write American music, and what better place to search for its roots than the northeast corner of Iowa? He could hear the land, expressed in the voice of rushing water, the wind, the birds. American music. Rooted in the urgent thrum of Indian drums, the sorrowful cry of Negro spirituals, the folk songs of early white settlers. Would there be Indians in Spillville? Then Tamás must come along—to take care of their instruments and to challenge his crazy idea.

Papio Tamás agreed because his daughter was sick with tuberculosis. Getting out of New York into fresh, western air would do her good. Mrs. Thurber, founder of the conservatory, urged Dvořák to go to Omaha sometime during the summer and visit her friend, Mr. Rosewater, influential editor of the *Omaha Bee*. Since Rosewater was a Czech immigrant, born a few miles from Dvořák's birthplace, he agreed to that as well.

When their train reached the village of Calmar, all thirteen of them crowded into three buggies for the five-mile drive to the hamlet of Spillville: Dvořák and his wife, their six children, his wife's sister, the family housemaid, Josef Kovařík, Tamás, and his daughter Sylvia, who was sixteen years old.

Spillville felt wild, Dvořák thought. But stimulating. He completed the entire sketch of Opus 96, the *American* string quartet, in the first three days, and wrote in his black notebook, *Thanks to the Lord God, I am satisfied, it went quickly.* Dvořák carried the notebook to record gifts that came by air:

the sound of falling water inspired the slow movement of his *Sonatina for Violin*, a scarlet tanager contributed the *Scherzo* of the *American* quartet. When he ran out of paper, he wrote on his cuffs or the front of his shirt. Dvořák and Kovařík played duets, violin and viola, invited Tamás to join them for trios. They drank beer, ate rye bread with salt.

The Indians came at the end of summer, a small band hawking medicinal herbs. The leader, Big Moon the arrowmaker, cured Dvořák's headache with snake oil. They sold blood medicine, gave a show every night, dancing, drumming, singing. Dvořák never missed a performance. To his delight, a minstrel show followed the Indians, black musicians singing to guitars and banjos. He thanked God and Josef Kovařík for leading him to Spillville. What a gift of Providence, to exhibit in one place the Indian and Negro roots of American music!

Over a pitcher of beer, he confided to Tamás, "The music of Negroes and Indians is virtually identical," and picked out similar pentatonic themes and resemblances of syncopation, as well as a tendency to flatten the seventh note of the scale. Tamás shook his head and observed the same type of syncopation could be found in Slovak and Hungarian music. And the flat seventh—there were plenty in Moravian and Slovak folksongs, not to speak of the early music of Dvořák. Displeased by this observation, the maestro thrust out his whiskers, replied, "There's an old Czech saying. Don't tell your grandmother how to churn butter!"

He waited until September to visit Omaha, leaving the children behind, travelling with his wife as well as Tamás and his daughter, who looked flushed, felt weak. They urged Sylvia to stay in Spillville with the children, but she would have felt anxious without her father, and insisted on coming along.

A crowd of Bohemians welcomed them at the station. The amiable Rosewater showed the visitors around town, promised festivities in their honor and a special performance by Omaha tribal musicians. Mrs. Rosewater tucked the sick girl into bed. In the evening, after a banquet in their honor, a Czech chorus sang folk melodies. Sylvia, missing the banquet, sipped broth, stayed in bed. Next day, Dvořák and his wife visited relatives of people they knew back home while Tamás sat at his daughter's bedside. In the evening, after another banquet, Dvořák and Kovařík played duets.

On the evening of the third day, the Indians appeared—my mother, accompanied by two drummers: my uncle and a man whose name I don't know. Sylvia refused to stay in bed. She wanted to hear the Indians.

To a European ear, ordinary tribal music sounds monotonous, rarely goes beyond the range of a single octave. The drum is everything, pounding its message with little variation of rhythm. Songs are not meant for solo performance—a chorus sings them in unison, and when people dance to the songs, the singers usually don't dance along with them. Mother was anything but an Omaha tribal musician. Her repertoire included many different styles, songs of Indians from eastern woodlands and the plains, as well as Negro spirituals and the folk music of white people. Dvořák was ecstatic. In the voice of one woman, he thought he heard the entire music of America.

As she performed for this group of white visitors, who came all the way from Spillville to listen, she explained in good English the meaning of what she sang. Not easy on the European ear, that music. Notes often sound flat or sharp with little change of pitch from one to the next, no sense of a melodic curve. Accompanied by the two drums, her rich soprano glided through Omaha birth chant, Algonkin praise for the dead, Iroquois dirge for the land, Caddouan war chant, Kickapoo healing ritual, sun greeting of the Yankton Sioux, prayers from Menominee drum ceremony.

After the Indian music, she returned them to familiar ground, sang a Nebraska folk song, *Farmer Needs Another Pig*. Everyone laughed. She concluded the program with a Negro spiritual, *Deep in the Hollow of My Soul*.

When Rosewater introduced her after the performance, Mother kept her eyes on Sylvia. Turning to Tamás, she said, "I'm a healer. Your girl is very sick. Let me save her."

Dvořák reminded Tamás how Big Moon's snake oil cured his headache. Tamás said nothing, wondered what to do. Sylvia spoke to her father in Romany, holding out her hand to my mother, who kept it between her palms. "I like her. Let her heal me. Please!"

My mother kept her from Death, healed her lungs. She felt a deep bond between herself and the girl. When she said goodbye, she threw her arms around Sylvia and cried, saying, "Death let me keep you, because some day, he said, I'll need you." For twenty-nine years they stayed in touch. Tamás and Sylvia went back to New York, and in the following year the Dvořák family returned to Bohemia. Sylvia grew up; Tamás grew old.

Thirty years after they met my mother, Papio Tamás and Little Mamo took me from my Omaha home to a new life in a new world. Made me their child. But before I say any more about them, I have to tell you about my mother's life before she met Dvořák.

2

She was born on the Omaha Reservation, about eighty miles north of the city, grew up on the west bank of the Missouri River, between the Middle Village and the Village of the Make-Believe White Men. When she was a child, her people still hunted buffalo, lived in lodges made of earth. As a young woman she was already a celebrity in our part of the world for her powers as a shaman as well as for her voice.

She married twice before she met my father. One husband was killed in a fight with the Sioux, and the other died because he drank too much. I was the only child my mother ever had. She ran away from my father just before she gave birth to me. I was born in a little frame house between the Reservation and the city of Omaha, in a tiny settlement of renegades and half-breeds they called the Hiding Place of Betsy Tom.

My mother was actually a granddaughter of Betsy Tom, a

half-caste and famous mystery woman of the Omahas with legendary powers—a shaman, healer, singer, and the leader of a dancing society. She never died, they say, but disappeared underground, where she remains in hiding. From time to time she emerges at night, usually in the dark of the moon, to do her work. When a sick person gets better without the benefit of Indian healers or white doctors, they say, "That's the work of Betsy Tom." Or when an ecstatic man dances as he never danced before, they say, "He's dancing with Betsy Tom." And when a beautiful song appears in the midst of the community, and everyone sings it but nobody knows where it comes from, they say, "That's a song of Betsy Tom." My mother was a shaman and a healer and a singer, like her grandmother.

Her father was trying to succeed as a farmer. The grand plan in those days was to stay Omaha on the inside but become white men on the outside. Therefore, when my mother was a young widow dwelling in the home of her father, she lived not in a traditional lodge made of earth, but in a new five-room wooden cottage overlooking the river. She met my father in that house. They carried him in unconscious, after he'd fallen off his horse dead drunk. He was an Army engineer supervising a project on the Missouri River. They brought him to her because she was a famous healer, and the house was only a quarter of a mile from the spot where he landed.

She nursed him through a concussion. When my father regained consciousness, she was leaning over him, and her raven hair, gathered in two stout braids, tickled his bare chest. He saw her bright eyes gazing down at him, felt her hand on his forehead, and said, "Damn good horse. He deserves a drink."

Father didn't hasten to recover. Gradually, he moved in his belongings, including cases of good whiskey. Even though alcohol was strictly prohibited on the Reservation, he never had any trouble smuggling it in. Her father—my Indian grandfather—welcomed him and the whiskey, encouraging this amiable, affluent white man to woo his daughter. My Indian grandfather was not a drunk, but he enjoyed good liquor. I think if he'd been a wealthy man in a different environment, he would have been a connoisseur. He called himself an explorer in the realm of spirits.

My father stayed in the house after she left him. "I'm a cage without a songbird," he complained. When he was sober, he usually stayed in some barracks. When he was not, he lived on the Reservation. His Indian father-in-law became his best friend. My Omaha grandfather called him his medium because through my father he could order spirits from abroad. With my father as a purchasing agent, my Omaha grandfather tried out different wines as well as exotic liquors from all over. My father remained content with a simple diet of whiskey.

He was a practical man whose parents had immigrated from Ireland, but Celtic witchcraft flowed in his veins. He recognized my mother for what she was. She captivated him. Love hit my mother like a July storm that strikes without warning and suddenly vanishes. In the eye of that storm, I was conceived. They were married by Omaha custom with a ceremonial feast and the traditional exchange of gifts. My father gave a horse and a case of Scotch.

Seven months after Father moved in, she moved out, repelled by his alcoholism and his instability. She refused to live with another drunken husband. And she refused to tolerate their conspiracy to change her. Grandfather wanted her to be like a white woman. Father wanted her to move away with him into the city. But she wanted to call up the spirits, to heal her people in the traditional way, to sing the old stories. Ironically, to do those things, she had to leave the Reservation and dwell in a settlement of mixed bloods and outcasts.

They welcomed her in the Hiding Place of Betsy Tom, nine miles south of the Reservation. Her brother rented a little shack for her and decided to live there too. He had lost his wives and children to the smallpox.

Proud to have my mother there, the neighbors would do anything for her. Two women helped bring me into the world. Josie Small Kettle was half Omaha, half white; Pauline Hard Walker a mixture of Ponca, Winnebago, Omaha, and white. As my mother sang holy songs and my uncle cut the umbilical cord, the two women held me upside down by the legs.

My uncle started to teach me things when I was still an infant. Then one day when I was about six years old, he put his hands on my shoulders and said, "Your mother does a good job of educating your soul. The House of Learning will take care of your brains. My specialty is the heart. I'll teach you everything about the heart."

When Mother left the Reservation, her people would not let go. They walked, rode, or were carried the nine miles to have her touch body and spirit. As sufferers from the city of Omaha discovered her, another stream of clients came up from the south. She didn't always cure them, but she saved some hopeless cases, and people say she never lost a woman in childbirth. She was also regarded as a medium and fortune teller. The waiting room gathered people of different races and cultures—

whites and blacks as well as Indians and mixed bloods—taking their common refuge for granted, peacefully discussing their afflictions and their hope.

I enjoyed prowling the woods, did not expect to like school. Stalking was my favorite activity. Armed with a tiny bow and grass arrows, I shot frogs and locusts. Every Monday morning, I walked about ten miles to attend the mission school on the Reservation, a large stone building three storeys high. The Indians called it the House of Learning. I lived there until Saturday afternoon, when I walked home. School was absorbing; I was happy there. Reading excited me, and I learned quickly. Before I knew it I sailed through *McGuffey's Fifth Eclectic Reader* and felt like the Columbus of a new world of books.

With boys my own age, I was in a gang we called Five Eagles. They made us speak English at the mission school and forbade Indian names. Every student received a new name. The leader of our gang was Daniel Webster. The others were Ulysses S. Grant, Millard Fillmore, and Theodore Roosevelt. Instead of using my Omaha name, Wathabezhika, which means Young Black Bear, they called me Mark Twain, because I told stories.

My first religious service brought me to the attention of the great Francis La Flesche. Anyone who reads Omaha ethnography knows his work. He was a friend of the superintendent and a frequent visitor to the school. As everyone kneeled to pray, the boy in charge of me pulled me down. On my knees, speaking loudly in Omaha, I demanded, "Why are we hiding like this? Who are we hiding from?" Everyone burst into laughter because the incident recalled a well-known event in the lore

of the school. They brought me to see him in the superintendent's office one of the days he visited. This huge, glittering
man, son of Iron Eye and the adopted grandson of Big Elk,
seemed to fill the room. He sat in the superintendent's chair,
dressed in a suit and tie like a white man, eyes black as a
crow's, smiling at me, trim mustache curled up at the ends.
The giant volume, The Omaha Tribe, which he wrote with
Alice Fletcher, dominated the shelf over the superintendent's
desk.

"History repeats itself," he said to me. "When I was a boy in
this school and we kneeled to pray, I asked what you asked.
Why are we hiding? Now I know the answer. We learn to be
Omaha inside and white men outside. But surrounded by real
white men, the Omaha within wants to hide. Study hard.
Learn to read and write and to think as the white men think.
Then you can stand up and say, No more hiding. This is my
world too."

After that he came in often to tutor me and loan me books.
The superintendent favored me as well, giving more books to
read and calling me in to talk about them. La Flesche introduced me to Alice Fletcher, a great anthropologist and a hand-
some, loving woman. She discovered I was the best singer in
the school, having inherited absolute pitch from my mother. I
inherited her memory as well, and I never forget a musical
phrase, written or unwritten. I can look at a sheet of music,
put it away, and perform it later.

Mother encouraged her clients to sing, gathered their music
in her head. She remembered every song she heard and taught
them all to me. Besides the Omaha songs, I learned music in
the other Siouan languages as well as songs of white people

and Negro spirituals. She taught me to compare music, showing me that Omaha singers played around with rhythm but kept the variation of pitch within a narrow range. Pitch interested her, and she experimented. Without knowing their names, my ear learned the modal scales. Since Alice Fletcher and Francis La Flesche were writing monographs on Omaha music, they spent hours with my mother, making a written record of her songs, taking notes as she discussed them.

Miss Fletcher heard me sing Omaha songs as well, and demonstrated simple patterns to me on the piano in school. Twice a week she came to the mission school to give me piano lessons and tell about the music of white people. I had no idea I was learning music theory.

One day when I was about ten years old, she brought in a violin. The superintendent remarked, "He's never seen a fiddle before." The violin fascinated me; I wanted to play it. After that, she took me to Omaha several times to hear the symphony orchestra. I resolved that when I grew up I would play a violin of my own in an orchestra.

My father moved into the city of Omaha and settled there, marrying a staunch Methodist woman who made him take the temperance pledge and stay sober. They never had any children. My uncle surmised that alcohol had destroyed Father's manhood, that it had taken all the power of Mother's witchcraft to raise his virility enough to conceive me. Three or four times a year, when my father came up to see me, Mother treated him with formal politeness, as if he were a distant relative. He kept offering money to help support me, but she always refused to accept it.

When I was twelve years old, my mother called me into her

bedroom one day to tell me she was going to die. She patted my hands as she held them in hers. "I had a nice long talk with Death," she said. "He's my friend. I was working on Dorothy Two Crows, who had another hemorrhage, and he agreed to let me keep Dorothy. But he said my time would come next year, and I would not be able to trick him out of it. He was very polite, telling me out of respect, giving me plenty of time to put my affairs in order."

I threw my arms around her neck. She cried too, calling me her only baby. "But I know your destiny," she said cheerfully, "and we have a lot to do to get ready. I have to send for the people who are going to take care of you when I'm gone."

She took me up to the trader's post on the Reservation, about three miles from the mission school, and dictated a letter. We both knew how to write, but sending a letter this way made it more solemn. Her friend, Mrs. McGovern, the wife of the man who ran the store, wrote down what she said, and posted the letter to New York City. "They're Gypsies," she told me. "You'll like them."

We waited for Sylvia to receive the letter Mother sent from the trading post. As soon as she and Papio Tamás arrived at our house, Sylvia took me in her arms. We all cried. "You're a big boy," she said, "but you're my new baby. I have four grandchildren and two daughters, but they all live far away. Your mother saved my life when I was very sick. You must come and live with me and my father." She was short and fat, roly-poly in a huge tent of a dress. Big hoops in her ears ornamented a round, brown face. My mother was tall and stately, and, I thought, very beautiful.

"Your mother is a big woman," Sylvia said, "a great woman.

You must call me Little Mamo."

Her father wanted me to call him Papio, which in Romany means grandfather. To distinguish him from my Indian grandfather, I called him Papio Tamás. That's how he pronounced it, PAWpio TOMush. He was a slim, little man with dark, slanting eyes in a brown, old face illuminated by enormous white eyebrows, a white mustache, and a great bush of white hair on top.

My mother didn't want me to be there when she died, so they packed up my belongings, and we said goodbye at the Union Pacific Railway station in Omaha. Five months later in New York, I received a letter in the handwriting of Mrs. McGovern, dictated by my uncle, informing me Mother had passed away. It was a curious letter. She had no disease, my uncle said. Death took her without leaving a mark.

3

Little Mamo and Papio Tamás lived on Vineyard Place in Brooklyn. Her husband, a Hungarian businessman, died of pneumonia soon after their second child was born, and she moved back home to keep house for her father. The garden in back was full of vines bearing little shriveled grapes that would curl your tongue. We gathered them in tubs, mashed the juice out, fermented the mess in barrels standing in the cellar. Papio Tamás cherished the brew not for its wine but for the stems and skins which contained silica and potash. He extracted potions that wrought magical changes in wood. Previously, they had lived in a section of the Lower East Side known as Little Hungary, but he needed a regular supply of grapes, and that's why they moved to the place in Brooklyn. I can't say for certain I lived in Brooklyn because inside the house we breathed the air of northern Italy, heard the echoes of

Cremona. My grandfather listened to Stradivari, but talked to Paganini.

The two-storey, green, wooden house had a covered porch upstairs in front on the second floor. In good weather, he spread unvarnished instruments out on the porch. That's why he located the workshop upstairs. Their bedrooms, living room, parlor, dining room, and kitchen were on the ground floor.

The parlor was reserved for visitors, but I would slip in to lie on the mohair couch or play on the green rug, and to gaze at pictures on the wall. One was a Gypsy wedding scene, painted by a Magyar artist, the other a faded copy of Jules Breton's *Song of the Lark*. A young peasant woman, barefoot and clad in a rough apron, blouse, and kerchief, with a sickle in her right hand, stood in the middle of a field. She had a round face, plump cheeks, and her lips were parted. With an exalted expression touched by surprise or wonder or delight, she gazed up and far away. The countryside was French, but Papio Tamás said the colors of the field reminded him of the Hungarian *puszta*, and the girl had the face of one he knew in the village of Pispökvác.

I had dwelt in Indian bungalows, and apart from the mission school, this was my first house with more than one floor. The upper storey was devoted to the workshop and storage rooms, but they fixed up a room for me next to the workshop, a room of my own on the second floor overlooking the backyard.

The first night after dinner, we performed a little ritual. Standing in the parlor, with the three of us holding hands, Little Mamo said very seriously, "Let's make vows. We take you as child, and you take us as little mother and grandfather. You give us your love, and we give you our ancestors."

I agreed, and we hugged, the three of us in a circle. Now I was a Manava, they insisted. Since my Omaha name, Wathabezhika, was difficult, they decided to use part of my school name, Mark Twain. I became Marko Manava.

Then Tamás picked up his violin and played a lively *csárdás*. Little Mamo took both my hands and we danced. When she played her own violin, I danced with Papio Tamás. We kept going till midnight. I fell into my new bed, too exhausted to think about my mother, asleep before there was a moment to cry.

The next evening after dinner they presented me with a violin. Not an ordinary fiddle, but a Gypsy violin. "We'll teach you the Gypsy way," Little Mamo said, "but you should learn classical music as well. I want you to have a *gadjo* teacher in the city." I loved it, and they encouraged, cheering my progress. Never before in their lives had they encountered such talent. Such a natural relationship to the instrument! I knew they exaggerated, but in that nursery of music, with such warmth and devoted attention, who could fail? My musical growth was inescapable.

"We'll give you a passport to the world," Papio Tamás said to me. "When you learn to play the fiddle the way we teach you, doors will open."

"You'll be as welcome as the Fool in the tarot," Little Mamo added. "That's a Gypsy saying that means welcome everywhere."

I started life over again, with music the amniotic fluid of my rebirth. The string players of the New York Symphony as well as the Metropolitan Opera virtually courted Papio Tamás, showered us with free tickets to everything. Each week, sometimes two or three times, I sat in Aeolian Hall, Carnegie Hall, the Met, absorbed in great music.

Half a block from Carnegie Hall, they opened the new Mecca Auditorium on 55th Street between Sixth and Seventh Avenues when I was about fifteen, and the New York Symphony moved there. The place appeared so beautiful to me, with its Moorish carving, two balconies, elegant lobbies, I felt transported to some palace in the Arabian Nights. When Paul Kochanski performed Ravel's *Tzigane*, Papio Tamás took me backstage, and the violinist showed me his famous Spanish Stradivari, inlaid with ivory in the purfling, with intaglio work on the ribs and scroll.

My first opera was Janáček's *Jenufa*, with Maria Jeritza in the title role at the Met. Her voice reminded me of my mother. Omaha children are taught not to cry, but my new self took over, and *Madame Butterfly* made me choke up and dissolve every time. Sometimes opera made me laugh. When a German tenor singing Siegfried stepped back through a cloud of steam, which represented the ring of fire around Brunhilde, and fell through an open trap door, I kept on giggling, even though Papio Tamás shook me, told me to shut up. Carpenters and electricians carried the tenor back up to the stage. Overpowering my disrespectful snorts, he sang through the last act.

I saw Stravinsky himself conduct *Petrushka* at the Met. What I remember is the peculiar way he made a bow to the audience, a semi-circular wiggle of his body—and the funny way he shook hands with the principals.

The high point of my life in Carnegie Hall was the concert to honor the eightieth birthday of Leopold Auer. The hall looked like a greenhouse, filled with palms, shrubs, flowers. Auer, the most celebrated violin teacher in the world, was a little old man with bent shoulders and white beard. How he could play! With Rachmaninoff at the piano, he stood between his greatest students, Heifetz and Zimbalist.

They held their fiddles high under the chin, oh so high, probably the way the old man had taught them, but he didn't hold his own high like that. The three of them performed something by Vivaldi, I don't remember exactly what, but the final piece was a solo, a Brahms Hungarian dance Papio Tamás and I often played together. He scorched us with Magyar fire. If the old man could only keep playing, I thought, he would never die.

4

I loved the rich tenor sound of the viola. It reached into my soul, fed some profound hunger, released an inner spring. Taking to the instrument naturally, I played first viola in the school orchestra. Papio Tamás, who was a fanatical violinist, did not hear what I heard, claimed he disliked viola music. He called it crabby, somber, cranky. Since I was so close to him in everything else—at home, in the shop, on the violin—my passion for the viola gave me a certain amount of independence. That's one reason I chose the Primrose path. Grudgingly, he admitted I had what it took to become a virtuoso: long arms, a memory that never forgot a tune, and my flexible fingers.

My music teachers encouraged me to attend a conservatory, and for a year I went to the New York Institute of Musical Art. I enjoyed playing and learning, but felt discontented, not ready to settle into a musical career. I needed the roving life.

I sought out my father, asked him to support me through college, told him I wanted a career that would give me financial independence and the freedom to move about the world. He liked the idea, and I attended a big midwestern university, graduating with a degree in electrical engineering. My father then supported me for a few years longer while I established a small engineering firm. I also kept going back to my uncle, until he said he had taught me everything he knew. I worked hard in my machine shop, exploring the mechanical expression of my magical experience, invented and patented a number of devices that made me rich.

Deep down, I wanted to be a healer, like my mother and uncle. I moved east to attend medical school, but at the end of my second year, they asked me not to return. They were civilized physicians, the dean informed me, and my ideas of healing belonged to an era of savagery and barbarism.

After that, I wandered. Not only to find my roots in the Old World, but also to trace the paths of my ancestors. I found the relatives of Papio Tamás in Hungary and lived with Gypsies. Then, in Greece and Italy, I studied what the local adepts called *la vecchia religione*, the old religion.

5

I discovered my spiritual ancestors, the philosophers of natural magic, and their books led me to the manuscripts of Hermes Trismegistus. One of them, known as the *Picatrix*, fascinated me, but a crucial chapter was missing. My search for the missing chapter led to the library of a Greek monastery, and put an end to my antiquarian adventures.

In that library I met Ametra, pronounced AHmetra. Her name in Greek means *measureless, indeterminate*—because she was nothing *exactly*. She taught me the skills of metamorphosis. My uncle got me started, but she's my real teacher. And because of her, I'm a merlin. Don't get me wrong. I don't mean the wizard of King Arthur. A merlin is a bird.

When I first met Ametra in the monastery library and we chatted about Hermetic manuscripts, she drew me out. I told her about my life, how I was born in a little settlement of renegades near the Omaha reservation, how my mother's brother taught me secret wisdom when I was still a child, how I was travelling now, exploring the ancient European tradition, searching for the roots of magic.

"The tradition is not something you discover by yourself, like truffles in the forest," she said. "I'll give it to you."

"Give?" I wondered.

"*Traditio* means 'delivery.'" She touched my hand. "You'll get what you want."

I should have asked, "What do *you* want in return?"

She questioned me about my spirit guides, and in my own tradition we don't talk about them except to close spiritual comrades. To show I trusted her, I described my vision quest: the dreams, the long fast behind the waterfall, the ghostly appearance of the falcon. I told how falcons guided me through the lower world, how I needed a peregrine to give me strength.

She shook her head. "Not peregrine. You're a merlin." I felt too astonished to say anything. Laying her hand on my face, she observed, "Definitely a merlin." Stroking my forehead, massaging the center with her fingers, she added, "But your eye is lazy."

When the monk approached, she removed her hand. I had wondered how she talked her way into this monastic environment, where women were strictly excluded. Then, when the monk who served as librarian came over to our table with some books, I knew. "Here are the volumes you wanted, sir." He addressed her politely, setting them on the table. It was clear he thought she was a man.

There was no ambiguity in my mind, for I saw a dark, sultry

woman, dressed in good taste—a costume modest, yet subtly erotic. When the monk left the table, she smiled at me, looked straight into my eyes. She was trusting me to notice her trick: the power to cause split perceptions—for the monk, a man; for me, a beautiful woman. She had deep black eyes, so black they flashed glints of silver. As she moistened her lips and gazed into my eyes, her erotic energy made my skin tingle. Out of her body flowed a penetrating, exciting aroma—a braided odor with different strands: fragrance of the sea, perfume of a pine forest on a spring morning, the wet scent of an aroused woman's sex, and something else—something the body knows but the mind lacks a word to name.

She took me home to an island, a place Ametra called *Fluaria*. There are almost fifteen hundred Greek islands and fewer than two hundred are occupied. The rest are supposed to be uninhabited—at least by humans. Fluaria lies in the Northern Sporades, somewhere between Samos and the Turkish coast. Ametra said it was guarded by perpetual mist. All you see is clouds over barren rock.

She brought me there in an ordinary fishing boat, a wooden sloop about thirty feet long with a high cabin like a box, a huge tiller, and a quiet engine, operated by two men who remained silent the whole time. They motored away from the dock, raised mainsail and jib, stopped the engine, and we sailed out of the harbor on a broad reach with a fresh breeze on our port quarter. She spoke a few words to them in a language I never heard before.

"How far is it?" I asked.

Her laugh sounded like the whisper of a silver chime. "About 12,000 years," she replied.

From the sea, the island appears as an irregular line of tall rocks stretching a mile or less, crowned by low-hanging clouds. From every direction it looks the same, menacing rocks obscured by mist. There's no reason for anyone to get close. But when you come in from the north and know what you're doing, a narrow passage opens into a channel between the sea cliffs. The channel turns sharply to the left, then makes a semi-circle to the right. Ametra called the rocks on one side the High Wall and the other side, the Inner Rim.

A gull stood on the tall rock at the mouth of the channel like a sentinel. When we passed the rock going in, she addressed the gull in the same language she spoke to the men. The bird looked at us and opened its wings, bobbing its head. She placed one hand on my forehead, the other hand behind my head, smiled, and said, "You have a visual problem. Your eye is still asleep." I blinked, squinted, and she laughed. "You'll see," she promised.

Near the mist-crowned reef, the wind dropped to nothing. As the man in the bow lowered the sails, the tiller man started the engine. When the channel, a bottomless ditch between the lofty rocks, seemed to end, we turned abruptly west, coming at last into a little harbor and a lovely beach—the only way to get on the island.

The island was a valley, a large bowl suspended inside the rocky perimeter. I say large because it felt like a great expanse. I could not understand how so much land could be concealed within a reef less than a mile long. Ametra explained, "To outsiders it's virtual space, waiting to be sensed through the imagination. Now you can experience this place as it really is."

The sky shone clear above us, the sea air smelled fresh, and the trees looked bright green. They did not resemble the dwarfed vegetation of a typical Greek island—I saw pines, firs, beeches, sycamores, oaks, and species I could not identify. In the center of the island the Amber Forest was a thick growth of tall conifers—weeping pines, she called them. The trees have been weeping, Ametra explained, since her ancestress, who ruled for millennia, left the island a long time ago, and their tears dropped to the ground, hardened into amber by the sun. The forest floor was strewn with amber pellets on a carpet of pine needles.

When we walked, Ametra taught me to see merlins. She would look up, catch her breath, grab my arm. Merlins are a species of falcon, and falconers still fly them at larks. Fast, bold, and brave, the merlin is very small, a little smaller than a pigeon, but a superb raptor. It seizes birds larger than itself, not afraid to attack anything. I once saw a merlin fight an eagle that tried to steal its prey. In the world of chivalry, it was the lady's hawk—even the queen flew merlins. Maybe because it was friendly, easily trained, and sat lightly on the wrist. On Fluaria, the merlin was the ruling spirit of falcons.

My first day on the island, we saw a cast of merlins chasing a skylark. One mounted, stooped, and struck, while the other, flying below, lazily turned upside down and clutched the tumbling quarry with its feet.

We lived near the beach in a large wooden house with three floors, surrounded by empty cottages. It was built in the Greek style, with a balcony around the upper storeys. The top floor served as a library with shelves from floor to ceiling full of books and manuscripts, windows all around, and long tables piled neatly with classics in Chinese, Sanskrit, and Persian.

Most of the time we lived alone, but sometimes there were servants who appeared suddenly and unexplained out of nowhere, not ghostly creatures but young men and women, solid and vigorous. Everyone on the island was barefoot—including Ametra and myself. The men wore soft phrygian caps with curved peaks, colored shirts and baggy trousers narrow at the ankles. The women dressed in Turkish trousers, tight-fitting jackets in bright colors, and small embroidered caps. The tips of their fingers and toes were dyed red, and their hair hung down in a multitude of tiny plaits. They vanished as mysteriously as they materialized. When I questioned Ametra, she shrugged. "They belong here. You have a visual problem. When you don't need to see them, you can't."

She taught me skills to bring me close—to render my nature more like hers. One day, lying together naked on the beach, she took my hand and said, "Feel my hand in your hand...Feel my hand in your mind...Hold my breast...Take my breast into your mind...Let me in...Observe the beach...Listen to the rhythm of the waves...Smell the sea...Now observe your mind...Let your mind be the beach...Smell the blood as it surges through your mind...Feel the thoughts with your fingers ...Imagine a sea shell...Let the shell into your mind...Turn your mind into the shell...Be the shell...There, you're beginning to get the hang of it...Come back, come back, I don't want to live with a shell...Observe the island...Let the whole island into your mind..."

Sometimes she would get impatient with me, and I protested she expected too much too fast. In one of these fights I called her a vixen. She turned into a fox and demanded sex. I turned into a fox and chased her into the woods. We mated as foxes.

It was my first successful effort to change into the shape of a beast. Later, holding hands, as we walked the beach again in human form, she laughed, "I knew you could do it. But aren't you glad you didn't call me a hippopotamus?"

Her favorite name for me was *Gaidouri*, the Greek word for donkey. "Circe had to change her men into beasts," she said, pulling my ears. "You saved me a lot of work. You were already a donkey when you arrived."

Everything about her surprised me, but I admired her wide and profound learning. When I complimented her, she said, "You're such a jackass. You expect a sylvan to be stupid. You think I should be frolicking in the woods instead of reading books."

"Don't be absurd," I replied peevishly. "I met you in a library."

"Poor donkey. Were I not absurd, you could never experience me. My existence is absurd. *Quia incognoscibile sum.*" Whenever she laughed her little silver chime, I withdrew defensively. It was a maneuver she had taught—to close my inner gates and wrap them in white light. In another mood, her laugh could sound like the roar of a leopard. I preferred the leopard. When she imitated chimes, she was dangerous, and I was in for a rough bump.

She breathed into my ear, "Love me, Jackass."

"You're irresistible," I said as I held her close to me.

She chimed, "That's half your trouble. You think you have an obligation to resist. If you don't open up to me right now, I'll turn you into a pig."

My life with Ametra was tuned to sun, moon, stars, seasons. Her emotions changed like weather. Sometimes she was playful, or wept in melancholy. Other times she stormed, attacking me savagely. Her attitude fluctuated between devotion and mockery.

The climate was so agreeable we often slept under the stars on the green in front of the house, or on the beach, or in the Amber Forest. Every Saturday, the fishing boat arrived with supplies. Along with food and household things, they unloaded crates of books as well as magazines and newspapers, which kept her in touch with the outside world. Subtle presences kept the house clean and prepared food. The environment felt private and secure, and I soon got used to the endless voices, whispers, creaks, and rustles.

"I love this place," I told her.

"Yes, we all love it. You'll long for it terribly after you go. And we'll miss you too."

"I don't want to leave the island!" I exclaimed.

She looked into my eyes, touched my forehead and ran her fingers through my hair, saying, "*Ptochos gaidouri*, poor donkey."

One day I asked directly, "How old are you?"

She answered in a teasing voice, "Not gallant, my love, to ask a lady her age. How old do I look?"

"Twenty-eight, I would guess."

She passed her hand over her cheeks and patted her chin. "As long as I keep working, I'll continue to look young."

"Are you immortal?"

"Actually," she replied in a serious tone, "I don't know. The only way to find out is if I die. As long as I live, we'll not know."

Every third month, with the change of season, Ametra

presided over a banquet for ruling spirits. It was a royal event, with barges arriving all the time, unloading stately visitors who were announced by heralds. A large staff of servants, pages, and courtiers appeared out of nowhere to do all the work. During these quarterly events, while Ametra was occupied with affairs of state, all the chambers in our house as well as the cottages were filled with visitors, and on some occasions, they set up a pavilion on the green, resplendent with banners, fluttering pennants, and brightly-colored tents. Most of the visitors looked like beautiful women—or so they appeared to me. When I remarked how ravishing this or that royal visitor looked, she would giggle sometimes and say, "That's easy. She's reflecting your own fantasy. You ought to see her as I see her."

There were men in the crowd as well—that is, presences who appeared as men. All the visitors were introduced to me, but I lost track of names and relationships. She called many of them daughters, sons, aunts, uncles, and cousins. Hundreds of cousins. At the time I thought it was some system of fictive kinship, and when she presented me with a son or daughter I took it as a figure of speech.

After the banquet they would have a business meeting, a long report of atrocities and human threats to the places they ruled. It was followed by a conference on the condition of the islands. Most of the talk was of how to preserve them and cope with the human destruction of nature. They spoke in the Old Language, the original tongue of creatures and spirits, still the universal language in the islands, difficult to follow. I rarely sat through an entire conference, but Ametra insisted I pay attention, made me learn it as we made rounds together, healing the beasts.

Every morning we'd go to a clearing in the Amber Forest and they would come to us—birds with damaged wings, a wildcat with a sliver in its throat, a weasel with an infected eye, a badger with a tumor, a squirrel that had eaten a daffodil and was suffering bellyache. They would chirp or growl or hiss, but when you tune your ear and know the structure of the Old Language, your mind grasps the meaning. Their name for her was the Ladymother. Me they called *Donkey*. They picked it up from her.

The first time I heard it from them, I was walking alone in the forest, in broad daylight—not a time for owls to appear—when an owl fluttered down on a branch in front of me, blinked, spun its head round the clock in both directions, trembled violently, and said, "Please touch. I'm quiet. Let's be here together." That's the standard greeting, though it can also be rendered, "Let us share this space in peace."

I gave the formal reply, which simply repeats, "Please touch. I'm quiet. Let's be here together."

"Please, Donkey," the owl said, very disturbed, "where's the Ladymother?" I told the owl where to find her, and we exchanged farewells. "Hunt well," the owl said. "Live carefully. Get fat," and it flew away.

It was uncanny, her connection to their lives. In bed late one night, she shuddered, listened, and said, "A little one fell out. We'll get it in the morning." But the following night, she leaped out of bed, crying, "Another one. I must go to it right now. A fox is in the vicinity." We ran to the Amber Forest and picked a fledgling off the ground. She massaged its wings, rubbed the injured neck. "Climb on to that branch," she commanded, "and I'll hand it up to you." She breathed on the bird before I slipped it back into the nest.

She taught me to heal creatures—everything from snakes to polecats—but had no power to prevent death. Ferrets, martens, fishers, and wildcats prowled the island. I saw predatory beasts taking rodents, hawks seizing birds. Yet, I never came across carrion or bones. A creature that needed to die managed to swim or fly to another place. Once I saw the fishing boat come to take away a severely injured forest dog. "Why didn't you heal the dog?" I asked.

"There's a limit to what I can do," she answered. "He was too far gone." But she smiled. "You expect I can do anything. Then it's time."

"For what?" I asked.

"Time to open your merlin eye."

6

Early next morning, as the island stirred with creatures seeking breakfast, Ametra explained a merlin had agreed to adopt me. We walked from our house, near the east shore facing the beach, and skirted the edge of the Amber Forest to a swampy expanse north of it. In this stretch of open country, we made our way through bogs and patches of heather. Mounds of stone here and there loomed on the moor like islands. We tramped through green meadows, bare stony places, sticky bogs, and rust-colored sedge grasses bending in the wind.

She halted in front of a bank of rocks about twenty feet high. A merlin with dark-brown plumage sat on a boulder, gazing at me from large dark eyes on each side of her strong, curved beak. She was tiny, about a foot long, but in my awareness she felt as large as an eagle. The boulder, gripped by her long talons, was splashed with white droppings. We exchanged greetings in the Old Language, and Ametra, standing on my left, grasped the back of my neck in her hand and said, "I brought you my mate. He's only a human and has no power."

Feeling something move behind me, I turned and saw another merlin swoop down and perch on a hummock in the bog. He was a little smaller than the falcon on the rock and much brighter, with a shiny dark-blue head, a slate-blue back, whitish throat, and pale brown underbelly. He snapped up a passing dragonfly and looked me over. The merlin on the boulder said to me, "Are you hungry, child?"

Ametra held an arm around my shoulders, whispered in my ear, and I replied, "My belly is empty, Mother."

The merlin flew off the boulder and disappeared on the other side of the bank. As we waited, Ametra whispered, "Trust her." She slipped away and sat on a rock. Feeling a whir behind me, I turned and saw the brown merlin over my head. Gently she eased herself on to my shoulder. As she perched there, I felt the talons almost piercing the skin. She stared into my eyes. Ametra whispered, "Let her in. The way I taught you."

Lifting my attention into the gray mist behind my eyes, I felt the merlin inside me, then reversing the awareness, I entered the merlin. Ametra whispered again, and I said, "I'm hungry, Mother."

The merlin leaned over until I felt the feathers on my face. "Open your mouth," Ametra whispered, and as I obeyed I felt the beak inside it. I closed my eyes and expected to retch, waiting for a squirt of partially digested meadowlark or a casserole of moths. Instead, I opened my eyes, grunting with delight. "More," I said, "please." Something delicious trickled down my throat, and the name of it escaped me. I tried to remember. I thought of superbly prepared escargots, recalled an unforgettable evening when I discovered a little restaurant on the hill in Montmartre owned by a genius of a chef known as Petit Guillaume.

"Thank you, Mother," I sighed.

She addressed the other merlin. "Take care of your new brother, Jack." The morning sun burnished feathers on his back, and he glowed blue against the rusty marsh grass, yellow mosses, and dark-green rushes. "I'm going home," Ametra whispered, leaving me alone with the falcons.

"Hunt well. Live carefully. Get fat," the merlin on the rock said, and flew away.

"Would you like to fly with me?" the blue-gray merlin on the hummock asked.

"I would, yes."

"I'll take you over the island." Sitting on a rock with my back resting against a boulder, I concentrated, and we entered one another. As my body rested on the ground, my whole experience moved into the body of the little falcon. I saw the world through the jack merlin's eyes.

The sun had cleared away the mist, and butterflies swarmed on the shrubs. We heard a young buzzard crying for his breakfast in the trees at the edge of the Amber Forest. The merlin lifted from the hummock in a straight climbing flight into the trees. My stomach went queasy with the sudden feeling. When we reached a belt of hawthorn trees he began to circle, climbing in a spiral until we hovered over the forest. I laughed out loud. The island looked like a photographic negative, with leaves appearing as a white bloom on the trees, as if someone had ripped open a sleeping bag to cover the forest with down.

Imagine a vivid world without color, in which I perceived every detail in crisp gradations of white, gray, and black. Soaring high above the forest, I noticed birds, mice, and other creatures in the open spaces.

Eventually I adapted to the tumbling sensation of flight, and the dizziness left me. I enjoyed watching the horizon flip up and down, observing the sea and the island from all angles. As we traced the coastline, the island looked like an irregular bowl with the Amber Forest in the center taking up more than half the surface, sandy beach in the east, moor in the north, swampy ground in the west, meadows in the south, with a fortress perimeter, the double wall of sea cliffs.

We passed a family of buzzards on the soar, skirted a cluster of jackdaws tumbling over a hill on the far side of the moor. Plover and snipe skimmed over the beach.

Having toured the island in several directions, the jack merlin's attention strayed to interests of his own. We noticed a flock of pipits in the meadow and my senses—confused with his—flooded with the illusion of steaming coffee, bacon, and eggs. Seeing a crowd of starlings in the high grass, he flew hard in that direction, but they screamed in fright and rushed for cover in a dense tangle of blackthorn and brambles.

Then he climbed in a direct line and began to soar. The wind had increased. Near the beach, we observed a flock of ducks enjoying the gusty air, scudding round the sky, doing spins and bumps. They glided low with paddles down, as if to land near the shore, then tucked up their undercarriages to swing up into the wind.

As the wind diminished again, he seemed to search the sky.

A lark came off the ground, and seeing us, started to climb in a ringing pattern to avoid the falcon. The jack began to circle as well, following the lark ring by ring. Both merlin and lark strove for altitude. When the falcon gained height above his quarry, he would stoop and strike. We drifted downwind, and the lark must have sensed the merlin was gaining altitude, for it suddenly dived for the stone wall bordering our house. Down, down it fell, a distant black speck against the clouds. The jack pursued, making a great stoop across the sky, but as the quarry plummeted into the wall to hide in a crevice, he soared up again, giving up the chase. I sent him a thought: Take me back, and without me aboard you can do some serious hunting.

As I stirred on the rock, sitting on the ground and feeling my own body again, he flew away over my head in the direction of breakfast.

Back home, I described my adventure to Ametra. "The island seems so big," I said, "and so full of excitement. Yet it's inaccessible. Does anyone know about Fluaria? Humans, I mean."

"Of course," she replied. "And you'll meet them next month. On the equinox, we'll have a party."

"Who's coming?"

"The sorcerers. It's like a tournament—they're competing, and I'm the judge. They want to show off their lightning," she explained. "They expect me to observe their silly tricks and choose the best sorcerer. They want me to proclaim the greatest sorcerer in Eurasia."

"No witches or sorceresses coming?"

"They know better."

"Why did you agree to all this?"

"Because I have a sense of responsibility. You have no idea how the quality of magical thinking has declined. This generation is ignorant; they don't study the tradition. Think they can make it up out of their heads. All you need to play at sorcery these days is an inflated ego. I'll have the most pretentious of them together in one place. What an opportunity."

"What are you going to do?"

"Teach them the oldest trick in the book. It probably dates back to Pesh."

"I can hardly wait."

"Join the contest. Mix with them and see what they're like. You'll have fun," she promised. Her smile vanished as she added, "You'll learn something about the tradition."

7

On the evening before the spring equinox, they began to arrive—some in ordinary boats, others in fantastic vessels—sixty wizards of the highest degree from Greece, Italy, Spain, Portugal, Bulgaria, Turkey, Persia, Mesopotamia. There was even an Englishman from Glastonbury, two Irishmen, a Welshman, and a Scot. None of them knew the Old Language, but each spoke several tongues. Ametra asked me to act as host and to choose an official language. "Will everyone be content with English?" I asked.

That seemed agreeable, and I began to sort out accommodations, giving instructions to the marshalls, pages, and servants, who as usual appeared out of nowhere, dressed in brightly colored costumes. Some wizards helped by inventing and erecting their own tents, trying to surpass one another with grotesque designs and startling decorations. One tent wall displayed a fantastic blue tree with a ladder of copulating monkeys descending from the top branch.

Ametra made an announcement. Her voice was gentle, as if she spoke at our elbow, but it could be heard all over the island. "Gentlemen, the realm of Fluaria is honored by your presence. Tomorrow night, before the contest begins, we shall enjoy a banquet, a feast to match your appetites. And I promise you an entertainment you will never forget." The wizards responded with their own *trompe l'oreille*: the island rang with applause.

The day of the equinox passed quickly. Everyone turned to me as the seneschal, and I found no moment to catch my breath, busy all day making decisions, unraveling snags. Servants dismantled two walls in the house by removing partitions, which had been cunningly fastened together by hidden brass fittings, and stored them in a shed, turning the dining room into a great hall, and by evening, sixty wizards sat expectantly at five long tables. Ametra and I sat at the head of different tables, and the principal chef served the two of us himself with tasty soup, delicious porridge, and vegetable dishes flavored with exquisite sauces. Ametra never ate meat, and I had adjusted my diet to hers.

But the sorcerers were given a feast to match their appetites. Servants loaded the huge tables with trays of roast swan, duck, suckling pig, pheasant, prime ribs, and sizzling beefsteak. The aromas evoked sighs of desire, and when they heaped their plates and began to chew, the wizards groaned with pleasure. The servants kept pouring flagons of wine.

We talked about incantations and spells. The man on my right, from Iraq, debated the one on my left, from Italy, arguing across me. Should wizards get involved in warfare? They reached no conclusion. Should they go into politics? What about influencing the stock markets? The men across the table talked about the future of sorcery. Someday the tide will turn, and there will be a renascence of magic, they agreed.

Ametra's voice filled the room. "What a lovely occasion. Let us share the blessings of the equinox and celebrate the rebirth of spring. Is everyone ready for dessert? I have a special treat." The sorcerers murmured their delight. "Don't clear the tables," she told the servants. "Push all the plates to the middle. Everyone clear away a little space in front of you. Pass out the seeds."

Five servants walked around the tables with wooden bowls in their left hands. They placed a solitary grape seed before each of us—except for Ametra who now sat alone by a wall, dressed in a white robe with a crown of leaves and berries on her long, black hair, seated on a platform in an armchair with her feet on a stool, flanked by leopards, one on each side.

"Gentlemen, relax and contemplate the seed in front of you." Servants reappeared with trays of knives. At each place they set a bone-handled hunting knife to the right of the grape seed. I tested the edge of the knife. It was honed to the sharpness of a razor. "Gentlemen, behold the seed of mystery. From this particle comes a vine, and from the vine the Earth Mother brings forth an abundance of grapes. We harvest the grapes to fill our bellies with nourishment, and we make wine to fill our hearts with joy."

She paused and stood up, each hand resting on the head of a leopard. "Let us beg the Earth Mother to burst this seed tonight with the force of life, to bring forth grapes right now, before the time of harvest, so we may conclude our feast with the taste of fruit." She paused again. The great cats looked up at her.

"Let us strip every obstacle that stands between us and the force of life. Every veil must drop. Gentlemen, remove your clothing. As I do." She fingered the clasp at her throat and the robe dropped away. We gasped—even I, who knew her lovely body so intimately. We stared at the smooth flesh of her abdomen, the perfect lines of her hips, the dark triangle between her thighs, the full and rising breasts with nipples like berries. The men on my right and left were stunned. The two Irishmen at the next table seemed embarrassed. Many appeared puzzled. A few leered at one another—their expressions asking, was the archnymph of Fluaria going to do something lewd? Most stood fascinated.

As we stared at her breasts, they multiplied before our eyes. From collar to groin, her torso was covered with breasts. Once again she commanded, "Gentlemen, please remove your clothes." Hastily, we pulled off smocks, shirts, trousers, undergarments, and stood at the tables, naked. "Sit down at your places and concentrate on the seed before you."

The grape seed began to swell. It burst, and a green tendril crawled out of it. The little vine expanded and grew a branch on which buds appeared, changing into tiny globes, growing larger until each of us faced a cluster of luscious grapes. Everyone gasped, hummed, or murmured. Hands clapped in admiration.

"Now, take the branch in your left hand and hold the grapes in your lap. Grasp the knife in your right hand. Hold the knife over the grapes. Touch the edge of the knife to the branch.

Don't cut," she ordered, "don't cut!" Her chiming laugh rang through the hall. A chill went through me.

We blinked and stared. There were no grapes. Every one of us sat naked, holding his genitals in one hand and the knife, ready to cut, in the other. I hissed between my teeth, "Treachery! Shame!" Then uttered the worst thing I could say in the Old Language, "Blood in your face!" She looked straight at me, eyebrows furrowed in an expression of pain.

"Gentlemen," she said, "you have been deceived by the oldest trick in the annals of sorcery. Perhaps now you will study the tradition." A female servant placed the robe around her shoulders, and once again the long gown covered her body. We scrambled for our clothes. "The first rule of sorcery is to avoid being deceived!"

"What do you expect from us, Ladymother?" asked the Scot. "We're only men. We're not supernatural entities."

"I know you're not spirits. But I expect you to know your own history. Your spiritual ancestors were men. They performed the grape trick—didn't fall for it. How I miss the old sorcerers! A great one like Opicinus performed the grape trick in the highest circles." Ametra sat on her throne again, garbed in shining white. "Until you change your ways," she scolded, "you'll stay victims of your own fantasies."

The remains of the feast left on the plates in the middle of the tables began to disintegrate before our eyes. Swan carcasses turned into pieces of driftwood. Chunks of meat and bone dissolved into stones, twigs, bundles of grass, and lumps of mud. The entire feast was an illusion. Some of the guests vomited on the floor, liquid messes of gravel, slivers, fiber.

Silently, the wizards left the hall. They struck tents, packed bags, tied up boxes, climbed aboard their vessels, and slipped away into the mist.

Ametra and I walked on the beach while the great hall was cleared, the walls restored, rooms mopped, cottages tidied up, and the green swept clear. The moon was full, almost directly overhead. "Yes," I admitted, "that's what I said. I felt you had death in your heart." She was no longer like a goddess or a queen, but simply the woman I lived with.

She faced me and tears coursed down her cheeks. "You don't understand," she cried, turning her face to the side.

We talked it out. For days we talked about her intentions and all the ramifications of what I should have understood. She assured me the threat to our manhood was merely a dramatic gesture, not motivated by hostility. She cherished my virility, would never ruin something as precious to her as it was to me. The sorcerers needed the lesson. And see what I had learned as well. While experiencing the power of deceit, I grasped the nature of illusion, penetrated the deepest layer of sorcery.

Under her spell, my anger faded. I expected love to flow back in like the tide, but the feeling between us was never the same. Having learned the first rule of sorcery, I could never trust her again. I strained to please, but the effort only made her look sad. What spoiled our love was not the quarrel, but the change in me. I feared she pitied my weakness, and I knew the womanly part of her struggled against pity. And perhaps she sensed I grew irritated by her arrogance, began to feel restless discontent. My apprenticeship was over.

I remember the night she told me. We were in bed, and I held her in my arms. After we made love, she lay on her back, one arm over her eyes, palm up, the other resting on her belly, palm down. "Rain trickles deep into the soil," she said. "I'm opening my womb to your seed. I want to have a baby next spring."

I sat up quickly. "You're getting pregnant?" She would not say another word. I fell asleep. Perhaps she would be more communicative in the morning.

Ametra would not talk about it until about a month later. She said it would be difficult for both of us, but I must leave the island and never see the child. We had a raging quarrel. "I want to take care of my child," I shouted.

"We're not talking about a human child," she replied, "the child of some woman who delivers in a hospital. We're talking about my baby. And I'm going to raise her according to the law."

"What law?"

"The law of my nature and the law of this island," she replied. "My child must never see her father's face. I shall raise her in the way I was raised—as a free spirit not subject to the power of any man."

"She needs a father. I had something to do with her conception, you know. It takes two to make a baby."

"Not necessarily. I have conceived before on my own."

"Parthenogenesis? Then why the hell did you get involved with me in the first place?"

"They don't turn out right."

"So I am necessary after all."

She grew calm. "Listen. I have compelling reasons. History is on my side—human history. Men and women argued this way 12,000 years ago, and the men won. That will never happen to us here. Never."

"What will you do if I refuse to leave?"

"I'll put you to sleep and gently deposit you on Samos."

"You needed me for one thing only."

She cried. "I knew it would end this way, but what else could I do? I chose you because I fell in love with you."

I went into the Amber Forest and slept alone for a week. I felt presences all around, but never saw anyone. Music in the air and hidden voices never ceased. I heard rustling noises, and hands I never saw left food, fruit, water, oil, and wine in wooden bowls, straw baskets, clay pots, and terracotta beakers. I thought the whole thing over, trying to remember every detail. Perhaps she has been doing this for hundreds of years. How many islands are ruled by her children? At first I felt like an insect—trapped, used, ejected—but then told myself, why take such a view of it? Think of yourself as the consort of a great queen and father of a future ruling spirit! She's sending you into exile for political reasons.

When it was time to go, I felt calm. The fishing boat came out of the mist and waited for me at the dock, tended by the same two men who had brought us to the island. I held her in my arms for the last time, kissed her lips, patted her belly. "Hunt well. Live carefully. Get fat," I said. She smiled a little as tears streamed down her face. *Traditio* meant delivery. I got what I wanted, an apprenticeship in sorcery, and *quid pro quo*, she got what she wanted. After *quid* said goodbye to *quo*, she would deliver my baby.

The boat pulled away from the dock. She watched me, and I gazed at her until we turned into the channel. With open wings, bobbing its head, the sentinel gull saluted our passage.

As the wind picked up, one man raised sail and the other stopped the engine.

Perhaps I would never see my firstborn child. What would she be like, I wondered? I imagined her as a lovely sylphid, feeding the deer, running with the hares, riding on a bear. As I leaned on the gunwale watching the gull on the rock, and we left the channel, a seal popped up at my elbow, echoed my farewell. "...Get fat."

Before mist veiled the island, a speck shot out of the forest, grew larger as it approached, ascended in the ring flight of a merlin, mounted, stooped, reversed, soared overhead. I tried to lift my awareness, to merge with him, but my eye was no longer open. Climbing in spirals, he seemed no more than a dot, a period marking the end. My brother Jack was the last to see me go.

One man stayed in the bow the whole time and scarcely looked at me. At the tiller, the other man—who could have been a Greek or a Turk or an Arab, a swarthy man wearing a black sweater, sea cap and mustache—smiled and made friendly gestures. I spoke to him in the Old Language and he seemed to understand but never replied. "Are you Turkish?" I asked. He shook his head. "Where are you taking me?" He shook his head again. When we saw land and approached a harbor, I asked, "Samos?"

He smiled and replied, "Samos." When I climbed out of the boat, the man in the bow handed up my violin and a duffel made of sailcloth. It contained all my things—papers, several passports, money—every one of my possessions down to the last detail, with one little addition. A sea shell.

8

I experimented with different identities—not superficial dis-
guises, mind you, but a real sequence of shape changes. I needed passports and other documents, but when you have plenty
of money it's easy to acquire papers, and my friend in
Liverpool, Russell Flambard, produced impeccable forgeries. I
travelled as a Swiss doctor, a Turkish acrobat, a Chinese merchant from Hong Kong, and a Canadian magician.

When I returned to New York, the people I loved were
gone. Little Mamo and Papio Tamás caught influenza and died
only a few months before my return. My Omaha uncle perished in some epidemic the year after I left. I felt all alone,
deprived not only of my family but even of last farewells and
the comfort of proper ceremonial.

My foster family left the house and all their property to
Little Mamo's daughters. A lawyer asked me to come to his

office and handed me a package addressed in the handwriting of Papio Tamás. *To My Beloved Grandson, Manava Marko.* I didn't want to cry in front of the lawyer so I brought it to my room.

The package contained a small varnished maple box glued shut like the body of a violin. I inserted my knife, gently detabled it, finding two wads of paper inside, each tied up with catgut. Cutting open the first, I unwrapped a scraper made of the finest steel. A message on the paper read, *Take my sword. You are my successor.* The other paper had no message. It contained a gold disc slightly larger than a coin, its surfaces worn, the edges thin. One side showed a heron, the other a man's face surrounded by Greek letters, scarcely legible, spelling out the name *Diomedes.*

The coin was a legacy from Minugia's old mentor, Professor Raimondi. But that's another story, all about Minugia and Raimondi. I just want to say what my grandfather had told me about the coin.

If you ever see my relatives, Raimondi told Minugia, show them this coin. *Some day perhaps you'll travel in Italy again. Go south, if you do, go to Puglia. My family's there. Lots of grand-nephews and grandnieces, and cousins beyond reckoning. They're a strange lot and you have to know how to find them. They all belong to a secret society, call themselves Lairone because they fancy themselves herons. When they're initiated, no matter what their original name may be—Raimondi or Marcello or Panzani—they take the name Lairone. So Luigi Raimondi becomes Luigi Lairone—Luigi the Heron. That's because of the conspiracy, you see. They keep the old faith. They still worship the bones of Holy Diomedes. According to their mythology, when he disappeared into the Tremiti Islands—*

which used to be called the Isles of Diomedes—his companions turned into the herons that still live there, the sacred birds of Diomedes. That's why they take the name Lairone. They're sweet people when you get to know them—if you can forgive all those super-stitions. Tell them you knew Umberto Raimondi.

Minugia feared he was the last of the old masters, yet passed the tradition of Cremona to Papio Tamás, who delivered it to me. *Traditio* means delivery. Papio Tamás left me a scraper made from the blade of a saber and a gold coin.

The scraper and the coin are the only material objects in my legacy. You can't measure the skill in my hands, the music in my head, the memories in my heart.

9

I lost my bearings, and my work in life seemed like a distant memory. Too weak to do anything, I caught the flu, followed by pneumonia, and started to die.

I was lying in bed, enduring fever and delirium, when the door opened and a man dressed in black, a man with a face the color of ashes, walked into the room, carrying a medical bag. He pulled up a chair to the side of the bed, sat down with the bag on his lap. I had not called for a doctor and was out of touch with people altogether, so no one else could have sent for a physician. I knew it was Death coming to get me. I also knew what was in the bag, for my mother had told me about this trick. He would open the bag, and the dreadful stink of rotting corpses would pour out of it. The shock was intended to polish me off, my *coup de disgrâce.*

I felt insulted and angry. To think that when Death came for me, with all my cultivated powers and distinguished ancestry, he would choose a second-rate cheap stunt to push me off stage. The rage in my heart made me forget all about pneumonia. I would teach him a thing or two.

I changed myself into a skeleton lying on the bed, leaving him staring at the popular image of himself—a caricature of the grim reaper. Nothing happened for a minute or two, and I waited for him to appreciate the magical sophistication of my ironic move. He wanted me dead, so I obliged him with the appearance of me even deader than he expected, but it was also a mirror of himself. He responded by turning into a merlin.

This move signalled an apology and a gesture of respect. As a merlin he abandoned his deadly self to represent the guardian of my vitality. For a courteous riposte, to acknowledge his apology, I turned into a field mouse. It was a gesture of trust, representing a tender creature vulnerable to a predatory falcon, yet ironically safe, because the merlin cannot kill me, no matter what form I take. Suddenly the merlin turned into an owl.

I changed into a boa constrictor. The owl turned into a large elk, antlers touching the ceiling. I changed into a leopard. The elk turned into a lion.

I changed into Heracles, dressed in a bearskin, standing with a club over my shoulder. We glared at each other, the lion and the hero. I evaluated the moment as a standoff. A lion can kill a man, but in Greek mythology, Heracles slew the lion with his hands. Death laughed. I relaxed, felt elated. When Death laughs, it means he accepts a wizard as a playmate.

An ordinary shaman moves around a deathbed, sometimes with the entire community as an audience. He enters the lower world in a trance, dramatizes a struggle with monsters and demons, and the people follow his agony with great attention. That's his expressive work, but the purpose of all those antics is to make an impression on Death—to amuse him. When Death is distracted from his work, then the shaman may be rewarded, if he is lucky, by a release from doom. At the whim of Death, the shaman gets to keep his client.

Well, Death found me distracting, let me keep myself. I changed into a gym instructor to suggest I had given him a workout. He turned into a small boy sitting on an old-fashioned school bench, to signify he had learned something from me.

But I was more than a shaman. A playmate of the inner circle does not hesitate to take liberties with Death, even scold him, and I seized this privilege of my new status to lecture him. I changed into an art history professor with two slide projectors.

Look at what's happened to your popular image, I said. Five hundred years ago, artists represented the triumph of Death, painted great murals showing your power over everything. Today, no one cares. They let the dead slip away as if they go on vacation. They deny you an identity, and you don't even care what you look like. You must be losing your self-respect.

"It's time for you to learn a thing or two, Professor Wiseass." He sat in a three-piece suit with a dispatch case on his lap, taking a vernacular tone to show I was sounding pompous. "When have I ever been represented with respect, or even with accuracy? I take the rap for my kindred spirits. They do the dirty work but I clean up. Do I make war? It's the Spirit of War who causes the damage, and I pick up the pieces. I'm not the Spirit of Disease. Or Famine. Or Violence. I don't produce misery. I bring suffering to an end." I changed back into my ordinary self, sat on the bed to listen. "Use your head," he continued. "How does Scripture represent me? Do I ride alone?"

He changed into a cartoon figure of the pale horseman: a polo player dressed all in pale yellow-green, seated on a yellow-green pony. I thought of the other three riders of the Apocalypse, white, black, and red.

"It's true I'm granted the right to kill by sword, by famine, by pestilence, and by wild beasts. But all of them, wild beasts, pestilence, famine, and sword, cause plenty of mischief on their own. I'm not responsible for what they do. And it will be a sad day when people can't find me."

He disappeared, and across the room I saw a fantastic image, an enormous locust with human face, ferocious teeth, tail of a scorpion, but equipped like a war horse. I heard the voice of Papio Tamás as he sounded when he read from the Bible: *And in those days shall men seek death, and shall not find it; and shall desire to die, and death shall flee from them.*

The apparition vanished, and I lay on the bed, all alone in the room. Death had deserted me. Perhaps an hour passed. I felt weak, but the fever was gone, and I was beginning to get hungry. Yet, he insisted on playing the last trick. The door opened, and the doctor entered the room again, dressed in black, carrying his bag. He leaned over the bed, felt my forehead, and said, "I think you're going to get better."

Just to be on the safe side, as he crossed the threshold, I called to him, "I'm no Pesh!" He acknowledged with a smile, tipped his hat, waved goodbye. It was my first big encounter with him.

In my professional capacity as a healer, I wrangled with the Leech many times. Sometimes, over the body of a client struggling for life, Death would talk about my mother, recalling one incident or another. I questioned him about my uncle, as well as about Little Mamo and Papio Tamás. He said he had looked after them while I was away, reported their last moments, which—if he told the truth—were peaceful, but he refused to give me a scrap of information about what happened to them after death.

He's reliable, Death is, and belongs to us. Nothing in the universe—not gods or fate or anything else—is strong enough to cheat us out of Death.

10

I'll tell you the facts about Pesh. In the Old Language, his full name is Pesh Lo Ropodil Yak Mur Na. You may have seen his picture. Prehistoric paintings in the caves of southern France show him when he was young. He's the man dressed as a bison, playing a musical bow, dancing in the midst of beasts on the wall of the cave at Les Trois Frères. He's also the ithyphallic shaman with the bird mask and bird on a stick, head thrown back in an unnatural angle, lying between the rhinoceros and the wounded bison at Lascaux. He's over 20,000 years old. No one knows exactly how old. He's still alive because Death won't take him.

Pesh is the greatest shaman who ever lived. His healing energy has never been equalled, and with his musical bow he even gained power over Death. Did you ever wonder about the survival of humanity through the stone age? How do you think fragile, vulnerable mammals like us made it through the dangers of prehistoric life? Human intelligence is the usual explanation, but it's not enough. During the infancy of the human species, the power of shamans kept us alive, fighting diseases, healing wounds, teaching people how to get along with the beasts. Then, when humans shifted priorities to concentrate on material resources, to rely on technology for protection, the powers of shamans declined. Pesh Lo Ropodil is one of the old ones.

He even has the power to heal himself. Very rare. And so successful when he wrangled, he fancied himself a match for Death. One day he overpowered Death with his musical bow. He made Death dance. A whole community was dying of some disease, and Pesh wrangled for them. He backed Death into a corner and played his music, forced Death to dance. Pesh refused to stop, said he would keep playing until Death agreed to release the people he was wrangling for. He won, but since that time Death refuses to have anything to do with Pesh. And poor Pesh is so old he can't bear to go on living.

The picture in the cave at Lascaux illustrates one of his early schemes to die. Gored by the bison, trampled by the rhino, he's lying between them. The bird on the stick—shamans call it the soul pole—falls out of his grasp. You can see from the picture that Pesh's neck is broken. He has tried to destroy himself many times, but Death ignores him, and Pesh, if he doesn't want to lie around shattered or poisoned or whatever condition he's in from some clever attempt on his own life, has to pull himself together, heal himself once more, and keep going. Now he implores Death to forgive and take him away. But I think Death keeps him here as a horrible example to other wizards. When Death finally comes to take away Pesh, they say—I'm not saying I believe it, but this is what they say—it will be the end of the human race. So Pesh suffers involuntary immortality.

He went back to Siberia a few years ago because he knew from prophetic vision there was going to be a terrible explosion in a large chemical plant. He sat in that place and waited to get blown up, hoping for annihilation. When it happened, the explosion blew everybody in the factory all over the landscape. Pesh was in smithereens but still alive. Since Death won't take him away, his spirit stays right there at the site of the explosion. Some nights the local wizards can't get to sleep because Pesh screams for help to his brother shamans, howls for Death to come and get him. The wizards up there have a ritual now they call "Picking up Pesh." They go over the ground with a basket in hand, picking up little bits of tissue and bone. Each thing they pick up they ask, "Are you Pesh?" The idea is if they can gather just a patch of Pesh—enough to make a critical mass—he can use his great powers to regenerate a material body and get himself back together again.

Pesh lives in our old legends. We hear about him in the oldest story in the world, the *Epic of Gilgamesh*. He's the character they called Utnapishtim, which the Hittites, who lacked patience with the Akkadian language, later shortened to Peshtim. Gilgamesh travels across the waters of death to find Utnapishtim and learn the secret of immortality. The epic glimpses Pesh during a happy period, enjoying his freedom from Death, but the Babylonians got it all wrong. According to their story, the gods gave him immortality because he built the ark, saved people and animals from the flood.

The gods have nothing to do with his mortality or the lack of it, and nobody warned Pesh about the flood. When it rained for weeks, he knew from prophetic insight what was coming. He tried to warn everybody. His neighbors kept saying, "It's bound to clear up." He persuaded his children and grandchildren and a company of friends to help him build a floating container an acre in size. The rest of the story you know, except the flood didn't really cover the world. But it sure did a lot of damage.

Healers refer to him all the time. Whenever we have a hopeless case and a colleague asks, How did you make out with that accident? Or that leukemia? Or that cardiac case? We reply, Not a thing left for me to do. He'll have to go to Pesh.

And we use his name in our healing ritual as well, to keep us on the right side of Death. When a healer wins a case, he or she sings a last song over the patient and concludes, "With this song I make you free of disease," then stoops to whisper in the ear of the patient, "and keep you back from Death." After that, he or she turns to Death and says in a respectful tone of voice, "But I'm no Pesh!" Every wizard of any consequence knows about Pesh.

Intermezzo: Harold Child

I have formed during the last few years
such close relations with this best and
truest friend of mankind, that his image
is not only no longer terrifying to me, but
is indeed very soothing and consoling!
—Wolfgang to Leopold Mozart

1

Now you know about my early ups and downs, long before I settled in Vermont. These days I need a tame and quiet life. That's why I chose to dwell in Shadow Valley.

I gave you an honest description of my situation, but I did leave something out. In my early years here, to add a little spice during the concert season, I played in a community orchestra, drove to Cambridge every Wednesday and rehearsed. I enjoyed playing, but never felt entirely satisfied with my viola. I was like a man who loves his wife, but can't forget a passionate love affair he had in his youth.

There was nothing technically wrong with the viola I played in the orchestra. I like to find an instrument that's basically sound and modify it. I take it apart and trim or shape to suit my needs. Usually, in a viola, the ribs are too thick for my ear, and I shave them down. Sometimes I change the gradations of table and back. Then I harden the wood with liquid glass, and temper it with protein. My grandfather's formulas change the quality of sound by treating the wood with alchemical substances. As he taught me, I soak the wood in ethyl silicate, which dries like glass. When the wood is petrified, I treat it with a fluid suspension made from the shells of crabs dissolved in acetic acid. I treat the bridge, sound post, and bass bar with liquid glass as well.

Even though I owned more than one viola that met my requirements, I felt haunted by the instrument I had played in Liverpool. I would hear it in my head, during a rest when the strings were silent, or in the middle of a count, waiting for my cue, or in the split second before my bow touched the strings. My need to play The Destiny again was a physical longing, like hunger for food or yearning for sex.

The Amy Beach Music Library supported a full orchestra, the Cambridge Sinfonia. It was in an L-shaped building not far from the big intersection where Brattle Street runs into Fresh Pond Parkway, a fine-looking building, sleek with white brick outside, polished wood, warm drapes, deep carpets within. The entrance to the concert hall was on Brattle, the library entrance just around the corner. The director of the library conducted the orchestra. She was a composer and a cellist, who also commanded, coaxed, enlightened over a hundred musicians—freelancers, semipros, and amateurs. I sat in the viola section. Out of Shadow Valley, I was a different man.

I had the energy of a man half my age, and to make social life easier, that's the part of me I represented. I changed my name as well as my appearance. In the Boston area they knew me as Harold Child, retired physician and amateur string player.

The name of course was inspired by Byron's unquiet hero.

Harold Child was about fifty, a friendly man who retired early from his medical career as a heart specialist to travel, play music, enjoy life. A well-groomed sensualist, with wavy gray hair, smooth broad face—shorter, more athletic, younger than Marko Manava—and the pleased look of a man certain of his pleasures. I changed everything—my shape, even the color of my eyes—but not my ears, which remained immutable. Many years ago on the isle of Fluaria, Ametra would pull my ears and say, "You were already a donkey when you arrived." As Harold Child, I grew my hair long enough to cover them a bit, and wore a hat to distract attention from my ears.

At my audition, Mia Giraki, the conductor of Cambridge Sinfonia as well as director of the library, tested my mastery of the viola repertoire. Then she insisted on playing with me. On the stage of the concert hall, with the concertmistress and another player alternating parts on the violin, and with Gerry, the conductor, playing cello, we made a lively ensemble, reading through Haydn and Schubert quartets.

From the beginning, the connection between Gerry and me was charged with expectation, like the gaze of old lovers who meet after many years, each waiting for the other to offer a sign of recognition. "With a name like Giraki, you must be Greek," I said.

"My father came from Athens, but I was born in Connecticut, grew up in New York." She was a lovely woman, about thirty, I guessed, with the trim figure of an athlete, long dark hair wrapped in a single braid, dark eyes, the face of an Artemis. You know how some women capture your interest immediately. And from the way her eyes lingered on my face, I felt she was thinking me over. "Everyone calls me Gerry," she said.

"You're a fine cellist. Where did you study?"

"Thank you. High School of Music and Art in New York, then Juilliard—till my parents persuaded me to do something practical. They're both lawyers. So I got a degree in public administration and worked as a bureaucrat—until this job came along. The big thing in my life is I'm a composer, but I need to make a living, and the job is perfect, lets me use both sides of the brain."

After that, when she moved close, I backed away, afraid to get involved. The way I felt about her, if I made love to Gerry, there was no way I could keep up my disguise as Harold Child, and I couldn't risk introducing her to Marko Manava.

However, I did enjoy relationships with some women in the Cambridge Sinfonia, but don't get the idea I buzzed from fiddle to flute, pollinating the orchestra. I stayed away from married women, and friends who got involved with me felt they knew what to expect—I never misled anyone with false promises. But in spite of my efforts to be discreet, I gathered a reputation for dalliance.

A man expects love affairs to be secret. (I mean a decent, serious man, not the trivial kind who brags about his exploits.) He imagines a universe with two lovers and no one else. A man keeps love to himself. But a woman needs to talk about her lover, at least to a sister or best friend, and talking about him is as natural as making love. Talk begets rumors, and rumors marked Harold Child as a man on the prowl.

I liked to spend a pleasant afternoon or evening with a woman, but usually left before midnight. The illusion of metamorphosis requires light—I can't distort perceptions without light. In the dark, I revert to Marko Manava. Yes, I might arrange to keep a light burning all night, but I might also fall asleep. Shape shifting emerges from dormant regions of the self, from sources older than mammalian and reptilian parts of the brain. It requires active thinking in archaic sectors of the mind, and I need to stay awake to hold a shape. If I fell asleep in a woman's arms, Harold Child would have turned into Marko Manava. All-night stands were impossible.

The library was nourished by the Boston Area Music Consortium, the Amy Beach Foundation, and the Wynd family. Dulcie Marvell Wynd, queen of philanthropy in New England, had studied piano, and her twin sons were violinists, serious amateurs who played at the professional level. The Wynd endowment supported both library and orchestra. The Amy Beach Music Library grew fast, taking over the entire library of the old Boston Music Consortium, and developed an extensive manuscript collection. As Harold Child, I served as a consultant on Gypsy music, pretending it was a hobby of mine.

All the librarians played in the orchestra. The keeper of manuscripts, Laura Sturnell, an apple-cheeked violinist, who grew up in Chicago and held a doctorate in musicology from Harvard but looked as if she just arrived from the plains of South Dakota, served as concertmistress. I called her "Lark." Our viola section sat near the cellos to the right of the conductor, and it was easy for me to look across the stage and see the first violins. I loved to watch her at rest, fiddle in her lap, absorbed in the music, lips parted, gazing up at the conductor. She had a round face and plump cheeks, and I couldn't help staring, waiting for a familiar expression of surprise or wonder or delight. Her face took me back to Little Mamo and Papio Tamás, to our house in Brooklyn, to the picture on the parlor wall, Breton's *Song of the Lark*.

The way I stared made her nervous, even when I explained the source of my affectionate nickname for her. I tried to make friends, even gave her a framed copy of Breton's painting. She didn't put it up on the wall of her office, as I suggested, but didn't throw it out either, and the painting stayed propped up on the floor in a corner, as if she intended to hang it some day. Sometimes we stood at a manuscript table together, looking at unpublished Gypsy music. A subtle fragrance from her body, not soap, not quite perfume, intrigued me. But when I moved to get a closer sniff, she stepped away. We drifted in a ring around the table. Like a dance. Some inner rule of hers commanded an iron number of inches between us.

My best friend in the orchestra was Stan Kimball, who played double bass—a tall, slim, black man in his fifties, who ran a small workshop that repaired medical equipment. He also served part time as chief technician of the library's physical plant. "Are you an engineer?" I asked when Gerry introduced us.

"Trained as a machinist," he replied, "and worked in all kinds of situations. Spent a lifetime on the shop floor. Been through the mill, you might say."

Gerry added, "He's a genius with machinery. There's nothing he can't fix. And wait till you hear him play the double bass."

I often found him in the stacks reading music history or in the treasure room studying Duke Ellington manuscripts. For some reason, Stan didn't want to talk about books or manuscripts. He insisted, "The purpose of this library is to serve as a front organization for a damn good orchestra!" Stan grew up playing bass fiddle in jazz groups. "But I got tired of it," he explained. "I love good music." We became close friends. Of all the people I knew in the orchestra, I miss him and Gerry the most.

Sometimes, Gerry played first cello, but usually conducted. And sometimes I felt so absorbed watching her expressive face, flowing gestures, supple body moving like a dancer, I almost missed my cues. "You'd never expect her to be such a powerful conductor," Stan confided. "She's only a little woman, but when she steps on the podium, she's as big as the Statue of Liberty."

2

That was my life, divided between Marko Manava in Vermont and Harold Child in Boston. Perhaps you know enough about me now to understand my mixed feelings as I sat on the porch in Vermont thinking about The Destiny, warning myself, *Stay out of it. Don't get involved!* Maybe I would have heeded my own warning—if it had not been for the drowning in the pond.

Early afternoon on a bright clear day. As I cleaned up after lunch, a kitchen drawer fell apart in my hands, which prodded me about the loose board in the porch stairs and recalled the screen door with a rough spot that jabbed my thumb. Time to fix those damn things! I walked down the hill to buy hardware and the newspaper and a loaf of bread.

There must have been fifty people moving together on the shore of the pond. Two men carried a stretcher, walking in step with a gray blanket stretched over their burden. Suddenly, a boy I knew ran out of the crowd, skipping to keep up with the stretcher. He seized a corner of the blanket and thrust it aside, looking at the secret underneath, then swiftly threw the blanket back to cover it again. He merely looked and ran away. I don't know if he was relieved by what he saw. Or disappointed. Or enlightened. I felt the power of his impulse and wanted to do the same.

The men bearing the stretcher stopped walking, and a doctor holding his black bag leaned over the gray blanket. As he rose, turned, and faced me, my stomach convulsed. He was no doctor, and I knew what was in the black bag. Death stared at me, disguised in the portly figure and walrus face of Russell Flambard. He unbuttoned his vest and showed me a belly full of worms. From the edge of the crowd, gazing into my eyes, Death held out the palm of his hand. Stop! Stay back!

I guessed the stretcher held the body of a child I knew, one of the kids who came up the hill to visit me, and the Leech didn't want me to get involved, didn't want me to wrangle for the child's life. I turned around, went back up the hill. Why was the Leech impersonating Russell Flambard?

I tried to telephone Russell and heard the line was out of service. Then I phoned the Liverpool police, claiming to be a relative. They turned me over to an officer in charge of the missing persons file, and she switched me to Central Headquarters, where I spoke to a sergeant in charge of community relations. He offered to do some research, asked me to phone again in a few days. Eventually they told me Russell Flambard was deceased.

He died in an explosion that destroyed his workplace last

April. They never found the body. It was impossible to determine exactly how many perished in that explosion, which wiped out the entire block. How did they know he died in the blast? Because he went missing and the police interviewed his employees. One of them who lived with the deceased said Russell went back to the shop around midnight and never returned. No, there was no record of those interviews. The blast had been investigated, and the authorities determined it was caused by a natural-gas leak. Not a bomb. They were quite sure the Provisional I.R.A. were not involved.

Feeling stunned, I grieved for my old friend, Russell. In a day or two, however, I began to think of The Destiny again. Did the fake Stradivari so-called viola perish in the blast as well? Maybe I'd go to Liverpool and search for Kate Spaulding.

3

It took longer than I expected to pack my things, book a flight, lease the house. Allowing myself a month in Cambridge, I rented a room near the library in a house that took in students. I spent a day at the library reading about Mozart, and in the middle of the afternoon asked Lark how many string trios he wrote. She looked it up. "The E-flat *Divertimento* is his only string trio, at least the only one published. There's a fragment in G major, but it's incomplete."

I told her my Gypsy sources convinced me Mozart composed a trio in Paris for Rigo Manava, and I wanted to find it. "If the manuscript does exist, is there any way to guess where it might be?"

"Give me a day or two," she replied.

Much to my surprise, Lark phoned me early one morning, and after breakfast, I hurried to the library. In the treasure room, she looked through a computer printout. The leads boiled down to one dealer who lived in Cremona, a dealer named Beniamino Luria, who acquired a cache of Mozart papers. She had already looked him up, had a little biographical sketch ready. "My friend Monica at the Harvard Music Library knows Luria personally," she said. "She's been to Cremona, and buys Italian manuscripts through him."

"What's he like?"

"Clever, learned, and humane. He spent some years of the war in an Italian concentration camp, but escaped and fought in the underground against the Fascists. After the war, he served in Parliament. He's well known as an art dealer in northern Italy and as a benefactor in the Jewish community." She paused to look at some notes on a pad. "And something of an historian. He showed Monica an article he wrote about an eighteenth-century physician named Morgagni." I made a note of that; it might come in handy. I would read about Morgagni, so Luria and I would have something to chat about.

Lark typed a label for a file on Luria and said, "In Cremona he has a little shop, but that's only facade. Monica says tunnels lead from the shop to a warehouse of valuable antiquities."

"I'm going to have a good time searching for this manuscript," I said.

"We definitely want to acquire it," she replied, "and I think there's enough money in our budget." For the first time, she looked into my eyes. "Harold, if you find that Mozart manuscript, I'll come over and pick it up."

It took me a week to get ready. Stan, Gerry, and Lark wished me *bon voyage*. "Hurry back for the concert season,"

Gerry said. "We need your viola. Maybe you can do a solo for us."

"Yes," I promised. "I'll play *Harold in Italy.*"

SECOND MOVEMENT: HAROLD IN ITALY

*Riffing: Performing an improvised solo
passage. Any solo may be a riff. Probably
derived from "refrain."*
—Brother Wetpenny,
Concise Dictionary of Music

1

It was not easy to find Kate Spaulding. I flew from Boston to London, stayed overnight, took the train to Liverpool, travelled light, carrying nothing but a cheap viola and one duffel bag. This viola was part of a scheme to get The Destiny through customs.

I had shopped in Boston and New York, locating just the right instrument, a large inexpensive viola that looked good. I found it in Smoky Simon's, a large music store in Brooklyn. The viola sounded awful, but in appearance was not a bad copy of the 1731 Strad Paganini owned, with some features copied from the 1701 Macdonald—the most famous of all Stradivari violas. It was a contralto model—at least two inches shorter than the huge tenor viola I was hoping to borrow, but I thought it would serve my purpose. It even had the conventional fake label. Simon, the owner of the store, a decent man, wrinkled his nose as he took my money, and said, "I suppose you know what you're doing."

"My foster grandfather would have said I'm buying a duck," I replied.

Then I invented a travelling coat for the viola—a thick plastic film smeared on with a brush. It did not interact with the wood or the varnish. When I applied heat from a hair dryer, the plastic skin curled up slightly. Slit by a nail file, it peeled clean away. The protective membrane was almost clear, but gave the viola a dirty grayish color. My scheme was to leave the country with a customs certificate identifying my gray viola. I would discard it in England and return to the United States with Kate's real Stradivari, covered with plastic skin, disguised as the Brooklyn duck.

The legend haunting my boyhood occupied my mind, and the old stories came back, recalling Paganini's obsession, Minugia's adventures, the devotion of Papio Tamás. Would I be the one to fulfill the Manava dream and play The Destiny to the world? Before returning to the United States, I intended to make one stop in Italy and visit Cremona. I wanted to buy the lost Mozart trio, written for The Destiny, from the dealer, Luria. But that was not the only reason. I needed to walk in the footsteps of Papio Tamás.

I would go to England as Marko Manava, but in Italy shift to Harold Child. Years ago, Russell Flambard had given me the name and address of a Mexican printer in the South End in case I wanted something in a hurry. The man was a talented forger and fixed me up with passport and papers. This fellow specialized in documents for illegal Latinos, but knew his business, produced eveything I needed, down to fine details such as calling cards and stationery. I was prepared to roam Italy as a retired physician and amateur musician.

In Liverpool, I went first to the site of Russell's establishment. The entire block reminded me of London after the Blitz. I walked through an acre of broken stones, turning over lumps of debris, finding nothing I could recognize. Near Russell's house, in the Laughing Billygoat, I talked to the pub owner, the man I had borrowed the key from. He called out to his wife, "Gentleman from America, Love, inquiring about the explosion. Friend of Russell Flambard, he says. Wants to find Kate."

She emerged from the back, wiping her hands on an apron. "Yes, Love, I know Kate," she told me. "They used to drop in for a pint quite regular. No, I don't know where she is. May have left the city. Terribly upset she was. The constable might know. Willie Duncan. He knew them both."

The policeman remembered the investigation, had interviewed Kate himself. She was shattered, poor soul. Yes, he thought there might be an address somewhere in his records. She was going to live with a relation. Come to the police station at three o'clock.

He found what I wanted. Kate was staying with her sister in Manchester. I phoned and she invited me to come round the following day. I took the next train. Her sister was divorced and living alone in a semidetached house on a little street off Fog Lane Park in Didsbury, five miles from the center of Manchester. Kate was alone in the house when I rang the bell. "My sister works in the Town Hall," she explained.

I took her hands and said, "Kate, I'm so sorry about Russell."

She put her arms around me, and I felt her body shake. "Marko, I didn't think I could cry any more," she said. "Thought there was nothing left."

She made some tea, and we sat on the couch in the living room. The rugs as well as the slip covers were light beige. An Afghan dog, the same color as the furnishings, stepped into the room, looked at us, lay down in a corner.

"You thought I was his girlfriend," she said as she poured the tea. I nodded. "We were married." I probably looked surprised. "Four years ago. Russell didn't want anyone to know. He talked about enemies. Said they could get at him through me if they knew I was his wife." She began to cry again. I held her hand. "Now I'm his widow." I kept silent while she recovered composure.

"Kate, who did it? Who blew the place up? Was it the I.R.A.?"

She wiped her eyes with a handkerchief. "Russell did some work for the Provos but was on good terms with them. I really don't know. He told me he decided to stop working for some group in the Middle East—I don't know if they were Palestinians or what. He didn't like their politics, and they were furious with him. He worried because he knew too much about them but refused to tell me any more than that."

"And there's no way to find out? All the records went in the blast?"

"That's right."

My heart was in my mouth as I asked, timidly, "Kate, is everything gone? Was anything saved?"

She smiled. "The viola," she said. "I remember you loved the big viola." I nodded, afraid to say a word more.

"It's safe. I was keeping it at home with my other instruments. It's under my bed."

I can't describe to you the depth and intensity of my relief—as if my only child had been in a terrible accident and, by some miracle, had escaped unharmed.

She left the room, returned with an instrument. Holding it in her lap, she unzipped the brown canvas cover, opened the black case, lifted out a large viola. I looked it over from scroll to tailpiece, examining face, back, purfling, pegs, height of the bridge, squinting into the sound holes, fingering the eyes of the scroll. I pulled a tape measure out of my pocket and checked the length in inches from upper to lower bout. Eighteen and seven-eighths. Larger than the Medici-Tuscan tenor viola. Larger than any viola I had ever seen. I remembered how it felt to play this instrument.

I could hear the tremor in my voice as I asked, "Kate, I'd like to borrow it."

She replied, "You can have it. I can't play it. I don't want it."

"Kate, you don't know what you own here. I lied to you when I said it was a fake Stradivari."

"Russell thought you were amusing. He would chuckle and tell me, 'The bloke's daft, Kate. He fancies it's a real Strad—I can tell from his face. We won't shatter his pipe dream. Don't tell him he's an ass.' He had fun watching you play it."

"Kate, Russell was wrong. It is a real Stradivari. And not an ordinary one—if you can call any Stradivari viola ordinary. It's an instrument of great historic importance—a legendary viola. My grandfather thought it was Stradivari's highest achievement. It's more than a viola..."

Abruptly, she stood up. "Let's take the dog for a walk," she said. "I promised my sister I'd take him outside." Replacing the instrument in its case, she shoved it under the couch. Locking the front door, she led me to the park, the dog lunging ahead of us, straining at the leash. She yanked at him. "Stupid, vicious beast," she growled.

"What's his name?" I asked.

"My sister calls him Ashcan."

"Ashcan?"

"Ashcan the Afghan. She got him because he matches the color of her hair—same as the furniture and the rug. He's a disgusting thing with a brain the size of a pea. If you let him off the lead he runs away. And if you're not careful, he'll bite. Heather bashes him with a mop stick." We entered Fog Lane Park, and Ashcan tugged at the leash, pulling us toward the zoo.

"Kate, what are your plans? Will you live with your sister here?"

"Not for long. I'll stay till I can make up my mind. Y'see, I can do anything I want—that's the trouble. Russell left me a lot of money. I mean a lot. It's shocking. The insurance benefit is enormous, but that's only part of it. They keep rolling in—this bank and that one, and investments, and Swiss accounts. I can't absorb it all."

"Will you go back to school? Weren't you studying at the Royal College?"

"I was at Trinity. I don't think I'll go back. Perhaps I'll buy a shop in London—but what for? To make more money?"

"I hope you'll keep up your music. You're a good violist."

"I've got to get over this before I can do anything. I just keep thinking about Russell. Perhaps I'll travel."

We reached the tiny zoo in the middle of the park. Two foxes with shabby coats and glazed eyes paced nervously. The dog, trembling with excitement, lunged to the edge of their cage, hunched up, and defecated. "He always does that," she said. "The smell of fox makes him shit."

We walked round the zoo, looked at ducks and geese, and headed back to the house. Inside, I held the Stradivari once again. Tightening the bow, I played scales. "It's not made for an ordinary player," she observed. "Too big."

"It's not a viola, Kate. I can play it off the shoulder because I have long arms and big hands." I stood and set it on a chair straight up, fingering it like a cello or gamba or double bass. In the lower register it sounded like a cello. "It's a lot more than a viola..." I started to explain, but with an impatient gesture, she interrupted.

"Do me a favor and take the thing. All it means to me is painful memories. I'll give it to you."

"Kate, it's worth a fortune."

"Russell was right. You are daft. But look at it my way. I don't need a fortune—I already have more money than I know what to do with. And suppose you're right and it is a Strad and the newspapers get wind of it. They'll come snooping into my past and pry into Russell's business. I don't need that."

"Let me take it for a while."

"Take it forever. I'll sell it to you. Then it's all yours and off my mind. One hundred pounds."

"Kate, you're out of your mind."

"One hundred quid. Final offer. And no V.A.T."

That's exactly how it happened. Kate took the gray duck and I left the house with The Destiny in my hand. I owned it. I took the next train to London, stayed overnight, flew to Milan. Then I changed my identity to Harold Child, rented a car, and drove to Cremona.

2

I made the pilgrimage, treading in the footsteps of Papio Tamás, wondering how he felt when he visited those places, trying to imagine his meditations. First I saw the little house where Stradivari lived for a few years after his marriage. Then I gazed at a modern building erected on the site of the house where he dwelled and worked for almost sixty years. It had overlooked the church of San Domenico, but now the house and church were gone. Even his grave was gone. Across the street in the Piazza Roma, I read a memorial stone marking the former location of his tomb. When they demolished the church of San Domenico, they opened his family sepulchre and shifted the entire confusion of bones to a place outside the city.

I carried the Stradivari everywhere. No one paid any attention to me or the plain dark viola case except one old man in the Piazza, singing loudly to himself near the memorial stone. He saluted me with his cane and commanded, "*Buongiorno, Signor Suonare*. Play a requiem for Stradivari."

I ended my tour at the Stradivari museum, which still held the remains of his workshop. The place was empty, and the guard at the desk greeted me, "*Sia il benevenuto, signore.*" Still grasping the handle of the viola case, I walked through the large sunlit room, peering into sixteen cabinets displaying wood and metal tools, forms, models, templates, plans, designs, sketches, scraps of paper, fragments of instruments. All of them had belonged to Stradivari. Several other cases exhibited violins, violas, and celli, none made by the master himself, but valuable copies, every one. The only completed Stradivari in the room was the one I carried.

I spent the entire afternoon at the museum, photographing everything, taking notes, hoping I would find some evidence the viola in my grasp—or *so-called viola*—was built in Stradivari's workshop. I spoke to the guard. My grandfather was a luthier in America, I said, and visited Cremona many times to meditate on this collection.

"Ah, *signore*, that would be many years ago, before the City acquired these relics."

"Where were they before that?"

"In private hands, *signore*. The last owner, I heard, was a luthier named Giuseppe Fiorini. He donated them to the city. But I don't know the history. The one man in Cremona who can tell you is Signor Luria."

"Beniamino Luria?"

"*Si, lui stesso.*"

That night I stayed in a little hotel in the Piazza Mazzini

called La Cucina di Cremona. The room was small, dark, and seedy, but I wanted to be near the center of town. However, in the middle of the night, two men on my floor woke me up, banging doors, shouting to one another, carrying on a loud conversation in the corridor. I felt too sleepy to confront them. Tomorrow I'll find a better place, I mumbled. Before falling asleep again, I touched the viola case under my bed.

In the morning after breakfast I set out for Luria's shop. Standing in an archway that led to a hotel, I discovered it across the street on the Via Solferino—a deceptively modest store front next to a tobacco shop. To the right of the door, the window announced Stradivari Souvenirs. The window on the left said *I Tarocchi* and held a display of tarot decks. The door was locked and I could see no one inside. I glanced at the souvenirs, an assortment of plastic violins, models, plaques, pictures. Did I have the right place? This was petty merchandise. I expected to find a high-class dealer and connoisseur. Standing at the tarot window, I examined the decks, pulled out a notebook, started to make a list.

A woman came out of the tobacco shop, asked what I wanted. I said I was looking for Signor Luria. She asked me to wait and returned to the tobacco shop. I stood at the window, still inspecting the tarot decks. Soon a young man appeared from a curtain behind the counter, unlocked the door. I walked in. "Are you interested in Stradivari, *signore*, or the tarot?"

I smiled. "Both Stradivari and the tarot interest me, but I came to see Beniamino Luria."

He led me through the curtain at the back of the shop down a long corridor to an office lined with walnut panels, furnished with a stately desk, comfortable leather chairs, Persian rug.

"You have a visitor," the young man announced, "interested in both *tarocchi* and Stradivari."

"Actually, I came to talk about something else," I said as we shook hands. "The Mozart manuscripts."

"Ah, the gentleman from America," Luria said, and stood up.

"Harold Child," I said, and produced a calling card.

"I was expecting you. Ettore, I'm going to show *Dottore* Child around. When we get to the library, bring coffee."

I took to Luria instantly, a dignified old gentleman with a gray mustache, lined cheeks, gray hair slicked back. He wore a brown jacket with a handkerchief in the breast pocket, a dark red sweater buttoned like a vest. When he stood up he stooped a little. "*Lei suona?*" he asked, nodding at the case sitting on the rug by my feet.

"*Si,*" I replied, "*sono un brav' amatore di musica.*"

"A violist, I presume?"

"I carry a viola when I travel because I like to find people to play chamber music. It's a good way to make friends."

"You are welcome. We Italians have a saying, you are as welcome as..."

I completed his sentence, "*Sono come il matto ne' tarocchi.*" As welcome as the Fool in the tarot.

"Indeed," he said. "You've come to the right place. And you're a medical man as well. My daughter is a physician. Do you have a specialty, *Dottore?*"

"I don't practice any more, retired two years ago. I was a heart specialist."

"*Dottore,* you're just the man I'm waiting for. I'm about to offer you a bargain."

"The manuscript?" I asked hopefully.

"I want to sell you a museum," he replied.

3

"What do you know about Giambattista Morgagni?" he asked.

Something told me to take seriously my disguise as a physician. I decided to play along with Luria, scratched my chin, as if I were trying to recall scraps of medical history. I hoped I'd remember what I read about Morgagni before I left the States. "I know he was a great anatomist because the body has things named after him."

"Such as?" he asked. Was he testing me?

"Such as the sinus of Morgagni, the rectal columns of Morgagni, the Morgagni hydatids. Just the things I learned in medical school."

"A man of highest ideals, Morgagni, and an illustrious scientist devoted to research. But also a great teacher. When we go to Padua to look at the museum, we'll make a stop at the

University and visit the Anatomy Theater where he lectured for many years. Above all, he was a doctor. Come, let me show you something." Picking up my viola, I followed him down another long corridor. Behind that deceptive facade of shops on the street, displaying tobacco and souvenirs, unsuspected hallways led back to countless rooms. Walking on a plain brown carpet, we passed openings in the wall covered by metal grilles. He explained the contents as we marched by. "That one on the right contains nothing but clocks. Modern ones with interesting mechanisms, as well as antiques. All sizes, all ages. Most of them need repair. On the left there, two rooms full of automata. Engines of wonder. Mechanical toys, theatrical machinery. Some go back two or three hundred years. There's a working model of Pascal's mechanical woman, and believe it or not, I have the original Vaucanson duck, as well as working versions of his mechanical musicians." We passed one room that had an oak door instead of a metal cage. "That's *la stanza dei tarocchi*," the tarot room, he explained.

We stopped at a cage containing shelves laden with cardboard boxes. He fished a key out of his pocket, opened the gate, tucked a file box under his arm. "I have a Mozart fragment that will interest you," he said. I breathed a sigh of relief. Despite his obsession with Morgagni, he still remembered what I came for.

Locking the gate, he suggested, "Into the library, please." At the end of the corridor we entered a double door made of oak, and he snapped on the light. A library table stood in the middle of a comfortable room lined with books. There were no windows, but the overhead light was more than adequate, and three or four armchairs had floor lamps right by them.

Another Persian carpet covered the floor.

We sat at the table as he opened the box. "I want you to see this because you're a musician." Pulling out a stack of file folders, he extracted a sheet of paper. "People all over Europe consulted Morgagni. There are more than a hundred of his clinical consultations in print, most of them in fine Latin. He was an elegant stylist. The Palatine Library in Parma has twelve thick volumes of unpublished papers by Morgagni. This is the thirteenth." He chuckled. "Like the thirteenth tribe—lost but not forgotten. Some day I'll have to give up these papers. But not to Parma probably. I think they should go to Padua, where he lived most of his life, or perhaps his birthplace, Forli. Sooner or later I'll decide. This is the most interesting group of all his papers, I think. Look at this one."

He placed a sheet of elegant handwriting before me, and I squinted. "Let me tell you what it is," he urged. "Dated 8 October 1770. Monday, at the country villa of Count Pallavicini, near Bologna. It happens to be the clinical record of a professional visit by Morgagni to Leopold Mozart and to the bedside of his fourteen-year-old son."

"Are you serious?" I asked.

His eyes sparkled. "I have no doubt of its authenticity, and the beauty is that it's more than a medical report. It gives precious historical details." He adjusted his spectacles, began to read slowly, translating into English, sliding the words over his tongue as if he were tasting some delicious confection.

I was summoned to Bologna by the Count, his messenger expressing great anxiety for the health of young Mozart, who has been feverish for several days. The first summons came a month previously, a request to consult me about the father, who injured his leg last June in Rome when their carriage turned over and he lunged to protect his son. The leg will not heal, and the stubborn Salzburger distrusts Italian doctors. The Count, who reveres both father and son, promised to summon the greatest physician in Italy. Of course, the old fox instructed the messenger to tell me that, hoping flattery would speed me from Padova to Bologna. But the journey is almost two days, and the weight of daily obligations as well as the burden of my years pressed me to decline the summons.

Luria glanced up to explain, "Morgagni was eighty-eight years old. This all happened the year before he died." He resumed.

Then when the boy took to bed with high fever, Count von Firmian, Governor-General of Milan, and Cardinal Legate Branciforte, both of them patients of mine, sent their messengers as well. Under this barrage, my resistance ended. I gave an anatomy demonstration on Friday, then dog-tired, travelled Saturday and on the Lord's Day, getting scant rest at crowded inns along the way, arriving in Bologna Monday morning. Padre Martini, the boy's music tutor, was at the bedside, looking distressed. Mozart the father hobbled around in an agitated way with

the aid of a stick. Examining his leg, I found no frac-
ture, but the ligaments were torn and healing slowly.
The injury was complicated by rheumatic inflamma-
tion in both hip and knee. There was a long wound
on the ventral surface of the leg, leaving tender flesh
around the tibia. It was healed, but not in the right
way. I did not like the look of the scar tissue. He
used no poultices but treated the wound with some
white ointment supplied by his wife. The right foot
remains swollen. Since this northern bigot suspects
Italian doctors are poisoners, I prescribed a hot hip
bath thrice daily and let it go at that.

Turning to the son, I carried out a thorough
examination. "So you're the famous boy I have heard
so much about," I said. "I must hear you play some
time. Perhaps you'll come to Padova." The boy
looked at me brightly, his face flushed with fever,
and replied, "After you cure me, Doctor, I promise
I'll play in Padova."

Luria glanced up from the document, peering at me over the
top of his spectacles. "He did play in Padua, the following year,
eight months before Morgagni died. On March 13, he played
the wonderful organ in the church of Santa Giustina. I'll bet
Morgagni was there to listen."

He noticed me fidgeting. I was eager to get on with the business that brought me to Cremona, and much as I loved
Mozart, this biographical distraction made me feel impatient.

"I'll summarize the rest," Luria said. "The boy was suffering
from a heavy cold and bad cough. He had what a doctor today

would call an upper-respiratory infection and tracheo-bronchitis. Morgagni took a careful medical history. The father revealed Wolfgang was constantly ill with symptoms that must have come from recurrent streptococcal infections. Of course, Morgagni didn't know about streptococci, but he recognized the syndrome and speculated about its impact on the kidneys. Good thinker, Morgagni. 'Keep him in bed,' Morgagni said. 'Impossible!' the father wailed. 'I must get up,' the boy protested. And Padre Martini exclaimed, 'Tomorrow he must be in the Hall of the Accademia Filarmonica. It's like an examination.' Leopold explained, 'You see, Wolferl is proposed for membership in the Academy as a *compositore*. A great honor.' Indeed a great honor," Luria explained, "and essential to his career in Italy. Leopold wanted him to have the title because they were planning a new opera in Milan, and if the composer were known as a member of the Academy, that would give him the highest prestige.

"Morgagni left some medicine to relieve the fever. Leopold had been treating his son with Margrave powder, his favorite household remedy. The rest of the document is all clinical details. Morgagni concluded the report in disgust. He warned them to keep the boy in bed, 'but these people are headstrong,' he writes."

Luria put his spectacles on the table. "What a treasure!" he said. "But I'll have to part with it sooner or later. I'm torn by the struggle between my cupidity as a collector and my zeal to defend Mozart's reputation."

"I don't understand the issue," I confessed.

"Do you know what happened the next day, October 9, 1770?"

"No, I don't."

Luria stood up and searched the shelves, returning with Alfred Einstein's study of Mozart as well as the older biography by Otto Jahn. He held out his spectacles, aiming them at my chest.

"On 9 October 1770, Wolfgang Amadeus Mozart was handed an exercise in polyphony and locked in a room at the Academy. They gave him a traditional piece of church music—a *cantus firmus* selected from the plainsong antiphons—and set him to compose over this base line three upper voices in strict counterpoint. The old history books say he passed with flying colors, quoting Leopold's boast that his son finished in half an hour. According to Leopold, the judges voted instantly and unanimously to elect him to the Academy.

"That's a lie! The exercise in Wolfgang's handwriting has a note on it by his father saying the exam was written in the Hall of the Academy on October tenth, not the ninth. What actually happened is on the ninth, the boy wrote out the exercise, which was handed to Martini, who made some corrections. On the tenth, Wolfgang returned to the Hall and turned in a revised version, incorporating the changes. All the documents are there in Bologna, in the archives of the Academy: the original exercise, Martini's revision, and the final copy in young Mozart's hand. Alfred Einstein writes that Leopold's boast is a fraud, and Wolfgang had failed completely. That's a lie too!"

I broke in to ask, "What's the difference? Do we have to believe Mozart at fourteen could do anything?"

"That's not the point! My clinical document right here on the table sheds light on what actually happened. You see, the records of the Accademia Filarmonica say, *At the end of less* than an hour, Signor Mozart brought his essay and in view of the special circumstances it was adjudged sufficient."

Luria slammed the table with the palm of his hand. "All the loose talk is unnecessary," he exclaimed. "The hero worshippers want him to pass with flying colors. Alfred Einstein says he failed completely. But nobody asks: *What did they mean by special circumstances?*"

"I suppose they acknowledged his genius and agreed to waive the examination."

"No! That's not a circumstance." He slammed the table again.

"Well, what is?" I asked.

"Morgagni's clinical report explains everything. The boy was sick, very sick. He must have gone to the Hall in a raging fever, coughing and sneezing, with such a headache he couldn't think straight. I can't believe in normal health he would fail a test in counterpoint, this same boy who five months previously walked out of the Sistine Chapel and wrote down from memory the entire score of Allegri's *Miserere*. He knew his stuff. Martini prepared him. Mozart studied counterpoint with him, did the exercise canons in Martini's book. What kind of evidence do you need? About the same time Mozart wrote a polyphonic composition of the *cantus firmus, Cibavit eos in adipe*. It proves his competence in strict counterpoint. The boy was ill on October 9, and the judges acknowledged it. That was the special circumstance." He paused, and I tried to think of some way to change the conversation.

Luria continued. "But he recovered quickly enough. What vitality! A fortnight later, he was at work in Milan, composing recitatives for his new opera, *Mitridate, King of Pontus*, which is no flimsy piece of work. Can anyone in his right mind propose that a composer with the power to write music of that order was incapable of strict counterpoint?"

I shrugged uncomfortably, feeling I was confronted by a fanatic. Luria closed the file folder. "Don't you care about Mozart's reputation?"

"Mozart's reputation is doing just fine without me," I replied. Wanting desperately to get off the subject, I ventured, "You're a fastidious historian, Signor Luria. How did you get interested in Morgagni in the first place?"

He paused, thought for a moment. "I acquainted Morgagni for personal reasons while collecting letters by a distinguished ancestor of mine, Isaac Hezekiah ben Samuel Lampronti, a rabbi of Ferrara and a physician as well. My mother descended from the Lampronti family. He studied medicine in Padua, practiced in Ferrara. He's an important Jewish theologian, and I wanted to gather his unpublished work. He corresponded with Morgagni. They exchanged clinical letters, but the tone was warm and congenial. They were good friends and respected each other. That's what led me to acquire the Morgagni papers as well as the letters. I brought you back here to warn you about their historical value and their importance to me personally. The papers came with the museum, but I intend to sell the museum and keep the papers. I want you to know that, so you won't think I'm swindling you when you buy the museum."

4

"I never bought a museum before," I said, wondering where this would lead.

Luria chuckled. "I don't expect you to buy it on your own. I want to sell you the idea, so you can persuade the right organization. Are you familiar with the Vesalius Society in Boston?"

"Not personally, but I know some of the people in it. Their conferences are highly respected."

"They promote interest in medical history, look for ways to bring history into medical education. It's not an easy thing to do. Physicians and medical students have limited time and resources to study history."

"I've never been to any of their events, but often think of going. Just never got around to it."

Luria nodded. "That's why a fascinating museum of medical history is exactly what they need. Boston has several medical schools, and it will stir up a lot of interest if they import an eighteenth-century museum of pathology. But you must see for yourself what a valuable resource it is. We'll go in a day or two. Some of the automata need repair, and I want to make sure the exhibits are in working order when you get there."

The door opened and Ettore backed in, pulling a tea wagon. He set cups of coffee before us along with milk, sugar, and cookies. An old man followed him, crutch under the left shoulder, patch over the right eye. His right hand dangled, and the right foot scarcely touched the floor. He moved slowly, carrying papers in his left hand, palm tight against the crossbrace of the crutch. Ettore left the room, and the old man leaned against the table, setting the papers before Luria, who took up a pen and signed them.

"I'm glad you came in," he said. "Meet *Dottore* Child from America. *Dottore*, this is Salomone Rubino, my advisor and dearest friend. He won't speak, *Dottore*, but he listens. The right side of his body is useless." Salomone shifted his crutch, eased into one of the armchairs. "Looks like half a man now, but he's worth more than a hundred to me. He's my second father. Salomone saved my life when we were guerrilla fighters against Mussolini. The *Fascisti* caught us. Salomone was seriously wounded, but they tortured him anyway.

"Salomone, *Dottore* Child is eager to see the Museum." The old man grunted and turned on his side. "Sit a while and rest," Luria told him. "I'm showing the *Dottore* around." We drank our coffee. I told Salomone I hoped to see him later, and we left the room.

Luria drummed the manuscript box with his fingers as we walked down the corridor past the cages. "That's not all I collected on Mozart," he said, looking at me from the corner of his eye. "As you probably know, his older son, Karl Thomas Mozart, died not far from here in Milan in 1858. He studied music with Bonifazio Asioli in Milan and wanted to go into the piano business, but that never worked out. Never did much with music and took a diplomatic post, working for the Viceroy of Naples in Milan. Sad. But he had his father's piano, a gift from his mother, and he kept a folder of unpublished fragments composed by his father. Most of his correspondence appeared in journals published by the Mozarteum in Austria, but I uncovered a cache of his papers that stayed in private hands. Karl Thomas remained a bachelor, and when he died, a servant grabbed those papers and sold them to the children of Asioli, his former music teacher. They remained with the Asioli family until I acquired them."

"You have them now?" I asked, feeling a rush of excitement.

"Sold them last year."

Excitement turned into disappointment. "Did the manuscripts you sold include a string trio? A trio never published?"

"I'm not sure, but I expect it did. I don't have anything like that now."

"Who bought it?"

"Professor Saggio at the Scuola is building up a beautiful manuscript archive. Clever man, Saggio, studied musicology in Paris. He has a Paganini collection as well as the Mozart papers."

"Where?"

"Right here in Cremona. You should visit the treasure room in the Biblioteca of the Scuola di Paleografia e Filologia Musicale. And you must meet Saggio."

5

Luria returned the manuscript box to its cage and gestured
to the shelves. "Many of these things will find their way to
important collections all over the world. I pursue great minds
with my broom and dustpan, gathering odds and ends, bits
and pieces of their lives, scraps of the past. I make my living as
a scrap merchant, *Dottore*." We stepped out and he locked the
cage. Waving his hands at both sides of the corridor, he said,
"This is the dustbin of history."

We passed the tarot room, and I asked, "Are we going in
there?"

He stopped and looked me over, as if struggling with a decision. "I suppose you want to see the Cremona *tarocchi*—the
Bembo deck?" When I didn't respond, his face betrayed an
expression of relief. Turning away from the door, he led me
back to his office.

Luria drummed his fingers on the desk. "Would you like more coffee, *Dottore?*"

I set the viola down by my feet. "No thanks."

"You have many interests, *Dottore*. You say you're a medical man and a musician. I suppose you know all about the tarot as well?"

"I'm not a stranger to the tarot," I admitted.

"Aha!" Luria stood up, then sat down again. He sighed and looked into my eyes. "I'll be honest. You make me suspicious, Harold Child. What's the probability an American physician with an improbable Byronic name comes here to buy a Mozart manuscript, but just happens to want the Cremona tarot deck as well? How many people in the world even know about the Cremona deck? Who are you?"

"Just a traveller, a tourist, and I never heard of the Cremona tarot deck till you mentioned it."

"You tell stories like a gypsy peddler," Luria said. "Nothing you say now will surprise me. Why don't you tell me you have a real Stradivari in that viola case?"

The door opened and Salomone dragged himself into the room. To my surprise, he stood behind me with a hand on my shoulder. "Salomone, I'm being rude to our visitor. I just told him I don't have any confidence in what he says."

The old man spoke with difficulty, his voice a rasp deep in his throat. "Ben, if he tells lies, that doesn't mean he's bad."

"Salomone, you're never wrong. What's your intuition about this man?"

He squeezed my shoulder, and shifting his crutch, eased himself into a chair. "He's all right, Ben."

Luria stared at me for a long time. We said nothing. Then

his attitude changed. He smiled. "We'll summon an examination committee and check your credentials."

"As a physician?"

"As a violist. How about a quartet?"

"I'd love it."

Salomone rasped, "Call Sara. Tell her to phone Raquele and Isacco. You want to see them anyway."

Luria dialed the phone on his desk. "*Come va, cara mia?* Have you practiced today? Well, you'd better. You're going to perform again." He covered the mouthpiece with his hand and whispered, "My wife's a pianist. Used to give concerts." Into the phone, he explained, "No, darling, just for fun. We have a visitor from America who's a violist...No, I don't think he knows David and Miriam. They live in New York, he's from Boston. America's a big place...Yes, I know next week is Passover...Yes, I'll invite him to the Seder. Salomone likes him. Now what about the music? I know you haven't practiced, but you're brilliant...Let's make it this coming Sunday at our house...That gives you three days. And call my other sweetheart. Tell her to come home for the weekend and bring her fiddle. And tell her to bring Isacco, but he can't come without his cello. Okay? Yes, I'll be home around seven. *Ciao.*"

Salomone leaned over to me and croaked, "We'll have a good time. You'll see."

"You'll stay in Cremona a while," Luria announced. "Have you ever been to a Seder?"

"Yes, of course."

"Have you ever been to an Italian Seder?"

I thought for a moment. "No, I don't think so."

He smiled and sat comfortably, hands folded over his stomach. "There's nothing like it," he said.

"A very holy experience?" I asked.

He raised his eyes to heaven and intoned, "Chicken soup, jellied striped bass, sauteed spinach, roasted baby goat, stuffed artichokes, matzoh pancakes with honey, almond cake..."

"Too good to miss," I assured him.

Nodding at my viola case, he asked, "Why do you carry that around with you?" I explained I didn't want to leave it at the hotel. He asked where I was staying, and when I said La Cucina di Cremona, he winced. "We must do something for you." He looked at Salomone, "The poor man has been sleeping in La Cuccia." I chuckled. *Cucina* means kitchen. *Cuccia* means dog bed.

Salomone rasped, "Call Bernardo."

Luria dialed again. "Vecchia Italia is the best hotel in town," he assured me. "Old fashioned. Excellent cuisine, beautiful rooms. You'll love it. There's only one problem—a big convention of violinists. But the owner is a good friend of mine. Poor man, he has heart trouble." We waited. He spoke into the phone, "Signor Rossi, please. Luria speaking...*Ciao*, Bernardo. *Come va?* How's your health? I see. Well, we're all getting on, you know. Listen, I'm going to do you a favor. I have a visitor from America, a distinguished heart specialist from Boston. Give him a nice room. Just think how lucky you are. If you have a heart attack, he's right there. I know about the convention, but you must have something...Give him the bridal suite or whatever. I'm sure you'll be creative...I'm counting on you...And Bernardo, one thing more. He's a musician and has an instrument with him. Will you keep it for him in your vault? The big combination safe in your office...No, he's not here for the convention...I know it's against your rules, but you made the rules. Do it for me, old friend, make an exception...He's staying with you because he's a heart specialist, not because he's a musician...Okay, okay. *Va bene*...Yes, thanks. I'll bring him over myself. Salomone adores him. *Ciao.*"

He lowered the phone, spoke to me in a conspiratorial whisper. "Ordinarily he doesn't put instruments in the safe, because there's not enough room to hold them all. But it's a splendid safe. Like a battleship. And the hotel is full of musicians, so you can practice day and night. They'll all be doing the same thing.

"We'll have a good time. Informal. Sara, my wife, on piano. Raquele, my daughter, violin. Her fiancé, Isacco, cello, and you on viola. Just family and a few friends, people we love. Including Bernardo, if he's not sick of string players."

6

Luria drove me to the Vecchia Italia Hotel. Since Cremona is a small city, nothing in it is far away. We could have walked easily, but he drove up Corso Mazzini, which became Corso Matteotti, and in a few minutes we were in the Piazalle Libertà off the Via Dante. The Vecchia Italia looked comfortable, a grand hotel in the old European style. Rossi, the owner, greeted us at the desk. "I have a nice room for you on the third floor, *Dottore*. One of the violinists checked out unexpectedly. Family emergency."

Rossi was a dark, stocky man about sixty years old, medium height, half bald, with horn-rimmed glasses, wearing a dark-blue suit and black bow tie. The skin of his jowls and neck showed he had lost weight. He seemed low in energy, head down, shoulders stooped. "How are you feeling?" I asked, trying to sound like a physician.

"Not too bad, but tired."

"I keep telling you, Bernardo," Luria said, "you need to get away a few days. Stay in my place on Lake Garda."

"*Grazie*, Ben. Maybe I will. As soon as things calm down a bit." He stood behind the long, L-shaped desk in the lobby, the panelled wall behind him, pigeon holes that served as mail boxes to his right. Things are not going to calm down here, I said to myself, watching an agitated young woman standing at the far end. One of the employees, I guessed, because she stood behind the desk.

I had noticed her as soon as I entered the lobby. Never saw her before, but when she spied me carrying the viola, her face lit up as if she recognized me. She looked delicate, with long, tangled, brown hair, pointed chin, wistful smile, wore the uniform of the chambermaids. Her mouth worked as she stared at me, whispering some word over and over again. As froth collected in the corners of her lips, her eyes glazed. She trembled, her whole body twitching, and she swayed. I hope she doesn't pass out here, I thought. She's tarantic.

"Who's the girl behind the desk?" I whispered to Luria.

"I don't know," he replied, and turned to Rossi to find out. As we passed her, she kept her eyes on me, the smile fixed on her face, body swaying.

We entered the lift to go up and look at my room. "Bernardo says her name is Stella Lairone. She and her brother have worked here a couple of years. She manages the chambermaids. Her brother, Francesco—they call him Franci—is the head waiter, and sometimes drives the car for Bernardo. Nice people and good workers. The staff refer to them as *i Pugliesi*, the family from Apulia." With a chuckle, he added, "They come from Buca."

People always pronounced it BOOOka, as if the long *ooo* stressed the weird quality of the place. It's not the name of an actual town in Apulia, but I knew what he meant. The word *buca* means "pit," and *la buca delle tarantole*, the pit of tarantulas, is a generic term for some villages in the south, between the spur and the heel of the boot, obscure villages scattered between Foggia and Taranto, chronically infected with tarantism, where people remained devoted to pagan superstition. They have a saying in the Pugliese dialect, "Christ went down to hell to rescue sinners, but stayed out of Buca."

We found my room, entered, and Luria inspected it. "This is a good room. You'll be comfortable here. Don't forget to practice. And when you go out, leave the viola in the safe."

Back in the lobby, Stella was gone. Lairone, I mused. Not a common name. The word means *heron*. I remembered what Papio Tamás told me about Professor Raimondi's last words to Minugia. His relatives in Apulia were named Lairone. Herons were attendants of Diomedes, *therapeutae* of the divine hero. Raimondi's relatives kept the old faith, worshipped the bones of Holy Diomedes. A strange lot, he said, but sweet people when you get to know them. That was a century and a half ago, but maybe some of them were still around. Maybe I'll meet them, I hoped.

I had my eye on the restaurant, but lingered at the desk as Luria shook hands with his friend. "Take good care of his instrument." He winked at Rossi. "He may have a real Stradivari in that viola case."

"Who knows the combination to the safe?" I asked Rossi.

"Only me and my lawyer," he replied. "And Franci," gesturing with his head at the restaurant. "He's reliable. Like my own son."

Luria said, "I'll pick up the *Dottore* in a few days when we go to Padua and look at the Morgagni Museum. He's a prospective buyer. Meanwhile, come to our little concert on Sunday."

"Listen, Ben, I'll take you up on that offer to let me stay at Lake Garda. But allow me to return a favor. Padua must be two hundred kilometers if you drive up to Brescia on the autostrade. Your Opel is a good car, but take my Mercedes, you'll be more comfortable. Franci can drive you. He's a good chauffeur."

"That's the long way around, and I hate the autostrade. It's only a hundred seventy kilometers if you go by Mantua. But sure, we'll take the Mercedes. If Franci drives, we can relax and talk business. *Dunque. Va bene. A più tardi. Ciao.*"

7

I enjoyed a good dinner in the hotel restaurant, kept the viola by me on the cushioned banquette, observed Franci, the head waiter, who suffered an occasional twitch on the left side of his face. After dinner, I returned to my room on the third floor, hearing scales, arpeggios, and familiar tunes from the violin repertoire escaping through closed doors up and down the corridor. The string players were fiddling away, and I felt confident no one would pay attention even if I practiced all night. I felt eager to master this so-called viola. From my briefcase I drew out musical scores, études, and exercise books, including Primrose and my well-thumbed Kreutzer.

I opened the viola case, cradled The Destiny in my hands. The primordial instrument, the Voice of Manush! It glowed orange-amber with a warm inner fire. The high sharp ridge and precise corners made it look wide awake. According to

Minugia, Stradivari learned alchemical secrets from Mihaly, first saturated the wood in ethyl silicate—liquid glass—then treated the petrified wood with a solution of locusts dissolved in vinegar. I held an instrument with three voices, the code of living things built into its parts. In its proportions, the Fibonacci Series: mathematics of growth. In the chitinous saturation of singing insects: metamorphosis. In the petrified wood: perpetual form, triumph over decay. You can hear them all when it sings.

I fiddled around with my favorite melodic lines from Bach Inventions and Sinfonias, striving to capture different qualities of feeling—Number 3 in D major, swift and merry; Number 9 in F minor, trembling with anguish; Number 4 in D minor, liquid and serene.

Playing the instrument thrilled me, except for its lowest string, which sounded less than perfect. The C string had a subdued quality—just a trifle—even when I replaced it with new gut. But when I replaced the highest string, the steel A, with gut as well, it liberated the C. I reckoned the tension on the high side, caused by wire string, had suppressed the low. With all new strings, and a tiny adjustment of the bridge, The Destiny opened like a flower. And opened me as well. Every phrase fetched a memory or evoked a daydream.

At first I played it like a viola, going through my usual warm up: long bows, scales, arpeggios, broken thirds ascending and descending. To wake up my left hand, I turned to the first few studies of Primrose, then worked through Kreutzer No. 9 six times. Crossing strings from C to A, I needed a limber hand. Next, Kreutzer No. 12 to work on intonation and train my right arm to move the bow smoothly over the broad surface.

Even though it was larger than any viola I had ever played, the instrument felt light. I try to hold an ordinary viola as level as possible, but the extra bulk of The Destiny required greater extension of my left arm, forced me to hold it at an angle with my chin, slanting toward the floor. It also forced me to press the strings with the fleshy tips of my fingers, and in high positions keep them down on the strings to balance my left hand. I learned to take them off the strings in a light sidewise motion, a whisper of pizzicato. My fingers learned correct relationships with one another, sought intimacy with the fingerboard, practiced broken fifths and double stops. I felt like a boy again, struggling to master viola in the workshop of Papio Tamás.

After the warmup, I played Stravinsky's *Elegy*, a viola piece that always absorbs me—prelude and fugue with prelude again at the end—hearing subtle, complex textures I had never noticed before.

Finding the parts to Dvořák's *American Quartet*, I lowered the tuning a third, played *scordato*, tried the cello part of the opening movement. It brought back the story of the composer at Spillville, Iowa, his trip to Omaha, my mother performing for him, singing Indian music to Dvořák.

Then I tried a different *scordatura*, a third above viola tuning, played a piece by Vaughan Williams I knew very well, a piece I had performed on violin, *The Lark Ascending*, a rhapsodic flight up the violin register, soaring in rising cadenzas. *She rises and begins to round.* In my daydream, I flew back to the island to be with Ametra. *She drops the silver chain of sound.* With merlin eye, I traced again the ring flight of a lark. *Ever winging up and up.* How soon after I left did Ametra find another mate? How long did he last? And does my child—the grownup child I never saw—share the island with her mother? What does Ametra tell her about me?

I pursued *The Lark*, but the high notes flew beyond my grasp. Despite my large hand, broad span, long fourth finger, *The Lark* got away.

Hearing something in the corridor, I opened the door, and the body of a woman fell into my room. She must have been leaning against the door. Writhing and twitching, she sprawled on the threshold. I pulled her inside the room and shut the door.

She wore the uniform of the chambermaids, black trousers and smock, white apron. I recognized Stella Lairone, guessed she had been listening to me play The Destiny. I ran to the phone, rang the desk, and in no time at all Franci and a waiter kneeled at her side.

On the carpet, foam on her lips, eyes rolled back in their sockets, Stella lay on her back, heels digging into the floor, lifted her hips, moving convulsively, thumped with the palms of her hands, panting and struggling for breath. She was a *tarantolata*.

I felt her pulse—rapid and thready—observed her breathing—quick and shallow. The waiter, a skinny man with light blue eyes, leaned over to ask Franci, "*Lui è mago?*" Is he a magician? That gave me an idea.

I massaged her hands, then held my hand on her forehead, spoke in a deep voice. "Stella, hear me! I'm a powerful magician. You sensed my lightning when I walked into the hotel. You are in the circle of my protection. I have power over tarantulas."

She groaned, sat up, asked for water. Franci and the waiter

raised her to her feet. As they left the room, supporting Stella between them, Franci said, "You're a great healer, *Dottore.* I won't forget you."

8

Next morning I slept late, until the phone rang. Franci apologized for waking me, said as a token of his appreciation, he would like...if I didn't mind...he begged the honor of serving me breakfast in my room at his own expense. I accepted, asked for juice, a mushroom omelette, coffee, and headed for the bathroom, but before I could get into the shower, the phone rang again with Rossi informing me the museum visit was scheduled for tomorrow. "*Inoltre, Dottore,* a message about your Sunday concert." Concert! I had thought of it as my private audition to win Luria's confidence, not as a concert.

Luria changed the venue, Rossi announced, and we would perform in the music room of the hotel. Fine with me, I replied, and I would be down after breakfast to pick up my instrument, because I needed to practice. Why not have Franci carry it up with breakfast? Rossi asked. I felt a tremor of anxiety, but dismissed it. Franci knew the combination anyway, and could have made off with The Destiny before breakfast if he wanted to steal it. Surely I could trust him to carry it from the safe to my room. Besides, the instrument provoked a feeling of recklessness in me, irritation with its demands, impatience with the need for security. It inspired a wish to be free of its power.

I was still getting dressed when he arrived with the breakfast cart. He looked refreshed, appearing in an immaculate and well-tailored waiter's uniform with a black bow tie, hair slicked back.

"Good morning, *Dottore*, here's your *violino*." He spoke Italian with an accent, almost a Greek accent. The look in his eye reassured me, a look of worship. He would do anything for me. And any fiddle thief would know something about strings, would never call an instrument as large as this one a "violin." It would be useful to have Franci around, seeking ways to express his gratitude. I thought I might need an assistant.

He told me he came from Murgia, a little town in Apulia. Must be like Buca, I thought, the legendary pit of tarantulas, where people remained devout pagans. "Your breakfast, *Dottore*." He spread a fresh white cloth, set the table. The mushrooms were special, from Apulia. And he took the liberty to bake with his own hands two specialities of his own town, a flaky little pastry like a quiche, I forget what he called it, with spinach in it, and tiny crescent rolls flavored with herbs. The names he gave the rolls were spoken in Murgiese, his local dialect, and didn't sound like Italian words. Pugliese speech is not uniform, for it changes every ten miles. In Massafra, they speak *Massafrese*, in Cisternino, *Cisternese*, in Franci's home town of Murgia, *Murgiese*. I told him what a nice breakfast, and how thoughtful to take such trouble. My privilege, sir, no trouble, he insisted.

Rolling the cart to the door, he paused at the chest of drawers which also served as a dressing table. In front of the mirror I had set a row of vials and flasks containing reagents to shape the protective membrane—the travelling coat for my viola. I start with locusts dissolved in vinegar. When you expose chitin solution to ammonia fumes, it produces fibers like a skin, which I stabilize in a light thermoplastic resin. Franci stared at the array of bottles. I smiled and suggested, "That's my *farmacia*."

He nodded. "You're a great healer," he said. Turning suddenly to face me, his back to the serving cart, he asked, "Are you a magician, *Dottore?*"

Disarmed by his naiveté, amused by his deference, I answered in jest, "Of course." After that, when we were alone, he dropped *Dottore*, and addressed me as *Signor Mago*.

9

On the road to Padua to visit the Morgagni Museum, Luria and I sat in back as Franci drove Rossi's Mercedes. I was glad we avoided the autostrade, where cars zoom by at two hundred kilometers an hour, grateful Franci drove cautiously, with the needle steady at ninety. I noticed tension in his neck, sensed he leaned back, straining to hear our conversation. With a writing pad on my lap, I made notes as Luria told me about the museum.

The exhibits, Luria said, were based on the record of Morgagni's clinical observations as well as his great work, *Seats and Causes of Disease Investigated by Anatomy*, published in 1761, ten years before he died, a book that recorded hundreds of dissections. While Morgagni was still alive, two of his former students, skilled artists as well as surgeons and professors of anatomy, made illustrations. Antonio Scarpa provided drawings while Leopoldo Caldani sculpted lifelike models in wax. Morgagni insisted on realistic detail, even to representing exact faces and bodies. That's what gave the museum historical interest—besides ordinary people, actual princes, nobles, cardinals in various conditions of illness. Padua was under Venetian supremacy in those days, and a number of wax statues represented certain dignitaries suffering various diseases. The local Paduans, who hated Venice, must have loved those exhibits. One effigy represented Ludovico Manin, the Doge of Venice, with an abscessed scrotum. The Doge confiscated the exhibit because it tarnished the dignity of his office. He melted the statue but returned the wax.

After Morgagni died, Scarpa and Caldani engaged Jacques Vaucanson to make automata. Vaucanson was director of the silk industry in France and a mechanical genius. He invented the first milling cutter—the essential element of milling machines—and improved mechanical looms, but what made him famous all over Europe was his automata, remarkably lifelike machines that behaved like men, women, animals. He made a duck that quacked, swam, fed, digested, excreted something that resembled duck shit. And he exhibited musicians, mechanical figures that really played a flute, beat a drum.

Luria claimed the surviving automata were in good working order, and he had delayed this visit of ours until all their mechanisms were repaired, lubricated, checked. But it's not clear how many Vaucanson actually made for the museum. The series on the reproductive system was incomplete, missing the initial exhibit—a mechanical man and woman engaged in sexual intercourse (Count Gio screwing Anna Bagioni, one of his servants, local Paduans said). The Doge confiscated this exhibit, for reasons having nothing to do with the dignity of Venice, and kept it in a special room of his own palazzo. The second exhibit in the series, intact and working, was a woman (the same Anna, they claimed) with a fetus in a transparent abdomen, giving birth. The third showed a babe sucking her transparent breast, which revealed ducts pumping white fluid (the kid even looked like the Count, they insisted).

In Padua, we paused at the University, in the northern part of the city, so Luria could show me the famous Anatomy Theater, where Morgagni lectured more than two centuries ago, then drove northeast along the canal into the industrial zone, and across the street from a *palazzetto dello sport*, stopped at a low concrete building which used to be a toy factory.

Modern pathology began with Morgagni, Luria said, and this was the first teaching museum in Italy. But the University lost control of it. At one stage of its history, a circus acquired the museum, then sold it to a theatrical family who exploited the exhibits in a lurid commercial scheme. They kept the collection intact, more or less, but added new exhibits. After months of research, with the help of a medical student, Luria restored the original Morgagni collection, separating it from what he called *rifiuti*, the rubbish.

"Please go through at your own pace, *Dottore*. I don't want you to feel any pressure, which you might imagine with me at your elbow. Any questions, give me a shout. Franci and I are working in the junk room, sorting out the rubbish."

Pretending serious interest, I inspected the rubbish, took notes. Weapons, wax representations of murder victims, stuffed monkey, hide of a rhinoceros, penis of a whale, double horns of a ram, wax effigy of Siamese twins, skull of a wild

187

boar from Africa, collection of butterflies, human fetus preserved in a jar, two crocodiles from the Nile, devil fish, Egyptian mummy, reptiles in alcohol, hand of a man with blood vessels injected with quicksilver, wax models of anatomical parts representing brain, heart, lungs, reproductive organs. I moved on.

Luria had organized the Morgagni exhibits in three sections: specimens, wax models, automata. The specimens showed tissues, organs, bones illustrating physical changes related to symptoms. One glass case exhibited a sample of Morgagni's medicines: crayfish tails, frog broth, amber, borage, sassafrass, ground ivy, melissa, ants, millipedes, worms, asses' milk, medicated wines, Crato pills.

I moved on to the wax statues, about two dozen, uniformly clothed in gray smocks, except for the parts on display, where cloth and skin disappeared to reveal sick tissue. Having compared the exhibits with Morgagni's book and his clinical observations, Luria typed out cards explaining the disease process or identifying the patient. Neat gray cards. Some of the exhibits still had eighteenth-century plaques. *Old Wound and a Lead Ball in the Femur.* Underneath, Luria's card added, *Captain Julio Zanetti of Piacenza.* The next one said, *Fistulous Sinuses in the Abdomen,* with Luria's note, *Countess Adelaide Turco-Bongiovanni of Verona.*

A man in costume staring at me gave me a start. Real as life: Abbot Maroni of Spilimberto with a malignant tumor in the anterior part of the right temple. Another, looking more shopworn: His Excellency the Duke of Lavello, Prince of Naples, with a hereditary bronchocele in the thyroid gland. An intense woman with a lined face, distress in her eyes: Signora Anna

Maria Compostello di Bassano with a suppurated tubercle in the lungs.

A sallow face with a thin mustache: His Excellency Emmanuele Count D'Arco, Master in the Court of Her Christian Majesty the Empress Maria Amalia, with syphilitic fistula in the perineum communicating with the urethra. His Excellency lay on his back, legs spread apart, a large incision in his crotch exposing the path of disease. He stared at the ceiling with bleak, watery eyes, unconscious of indignity, indifferent to his fate. I moved on to the automata.

A genial-looking, round-faced man with smooth, rosy cheeks sat on a bench. The rake of Padua, Count Giuseppi Guadagno, a notorious lecher, sitting on a bench with his eyes closed, probably resting up from his exertions. I pressed a lever on his shoe. The count opened his eyes, smiled, rose to his feet, unfastened the clasp at his throat, drew aside the lapels, revealing himself naked under the cloak. His penis inflated, swelled, ascended, extended, curved up in a crescent until the glans pointed back at his face. Peyronie's Disease, the card explained, fibrous sclerosis of the penis, first reported in a paper by François de la Peyronie, court physician to Louis XIV. In 1743, Peyronie observed in a letter to Morgagni, *the syndrome is more frequent in men who give themselves up to the vivacity of their temperaments.* I moved the lever on his shoe to its original position, setting the count on the path of detumescence. He snapped up his cloak, sat on the bench, closed his eyes.

I activated the other mechanisms, watching the birth process in a transparent womb until the crown of the child's head appeared, then moved on to the next and witnessed a babe nursing at the breast. At the end of the line of automata I reached a coffin with an eighteenth-century plaque: *Process of Decay*. On the lid, the gray card said, *Chiuso*. For some reason, this exhibit was closed. Out of curiosity, I opened the coffin.

10

The late Russell Flambard, as he looked the last time I saw him, gazed up at me from his round face with great jowls, walrus mustache, rimless spectacles, still wearing a high collar, tweed suit, fancy waistcoat. Startled, I moved back.

"It's me, chum. What a look on your face. As if I'm some ghastly humgruffin." He climbed out, put on his bowler hat, leaned over the coffin to pick up a shoe. "Lost me polly." Then, with a sly look, he leaned over again and pulled out a black bag, dusted it off. "Must look professional," he said. If he were not so macabre, I would have felt amused—Russell, the grand master of sham, impersonating a physician.

As I continued to back away, he patted his belly. "A trifle fubsey, yet still active." I wanted to get out of there. "I do enjoy flamboyant gestures," Russell said, flicking worms off his vest. "You bring out the theatrical side of me. You'll admit my behavior is generally grave?" A worm still clinging, he picked it off with two fingers, offered it to me. "I take pride in details." When I shrank back, he held the worm over the edge of the coffin, rubbed his fingers together, and explained, "*Dermestes lardarius*, a skin beetle."

I understood. Since the Leech was using the form of Russell's body, he chose insects that would be feeding on his scattered remains back in Liverpool. He scratched his ear vigorously with a little finger, and with mock drama, like a conjurer discovering a rabbit in a hat, fished out another larva. "*Ptinus tectus*," he said ruefully, dropped it in the coffin. "All this talk about food makes me peckish. Fish and chips is out of the question. D'ye suppose anywhere on this dreary peninsula we can find a decent pub lunch?" Russell's most amiable voice.

"What do you want?" I whispered, still frightened.

"Mr. Get To The Point, are ye?" Leaning against the wooden box, he put on the shoe he had fished out of it and said, "I'm here on a delicate matter."

It unnerved me, even though I should have been used to it—Death in disguise, playing with me again, this time in the voice and image of Russell Flambard. "Y'know the viola I gave Kate, the big one? You really fiddled her on that deal. Hundred quid! It's worth a bomb."

My nervousness disappeared in the rush to defend myself. "I offered a lot more. She refused."

"Yes, chum, tell me about it."

"What you're implying is simply not true!" I fell for the bait, hook, line, and sinker, acted as if I were quarreling with Russell himself. "She wanted to get rid of it, offered to give to me for nothing."

"You're not the legitimate owner," he insisted.

I responded angrily. "If I'm not, who the hell is?"

"I want you to sell it," he said. It dawned on me, he was playing a little game. A maneuver to get The Destiny out of my hands.

"It's mine," I blurted out, with not the slightest inkling of how to deal with the situation. "I won't give it up."

Russell sighed. "That's what I thought you'd say."

I felt panic. Felt like a careless, reckless fool, dashing off to Padua, leaving The Destiny behind in Cremona. My instinct suggested a maneuver of my own. "Okay, I'll give it to you. Come up to Cremona and I'll put The Destiny in your hands."

Did I glimpse a look of apprehension on Russell's face? "Dinna be daft, chum. You know I don't play the thing. I'm giving you a chance to make a few quid. As you Yanks say, let's talk Turkey. Carry it for me to a certain shop in Istanbul."

Here's where I get off the playmate train, I thought. The Leech will have to get along without me from now on. He must have guessed my mind, because he said, in Russell's most cajoling tone, "Chum, I'm about to do you a big favor. In a few days, you'll be enjoying a visit from a lady you fancy. She don't know it, but the lady's got GTT."

"What the hell is GTT?"

He held the black bag in front of him with both hands, frowned, pursed his lips, affecting the look of a Harley Street physician. "Gestational trophoblastic tumor. Looks like a bunch of grapes in the uterus. She'll think she's pregnant, but it's choriocarcinoma. No symptoms except the signs of pregnancy. A good gynecologist will pick it up—no fetal heartbeat, abnormal elevation of HCG in the blood sample. A sonogram

will confirm the tumor. It begins as a seed, turns into a cluster—a very invasive cancer, metastasizes fast, but with early diagnosis and swift intervention, she'll recover."

I could hear Luria and Franci finishing up in the junk room.
They closed the door. Footsteps. Pulling up his belt, Russell
said, "Excuse me while I go spend a penny." Before he disappeared round a corner, he turned back, winked. "You owe me
a favor, chum."

They came up to the side of the coffin, and Luria said, "We
heard you out here. Were you talking to the automata or to
yourself?"

"Talking to the dead," I replied.

Glancing back at the statues, Luria said, "They do look real,
don't they?"

On the road back to Cremona, Luria spoke and I kept
silent, mentally reviewing the encounter with Death. Who was
the lady in question? I tried to remember every woman I spoke
to since my arrival in England, was not aware of feeling attract-
ed to any, concluded he meant someone I was about to meet.

"Let's begin with a figure of seventy-five thousand dollars,"
Luria offered. "Very reasonable. Maybe you can become a
member of the Vesalius Society when you get back to Boston.
They'll take you seriously. Morgagni's collection is not only a
working museum but an historical monument and a valuable
resource. It really shouldn't leave Italy." Taking my silence for a
bargaining maneuver, he lowered the price, until he reached
sixty-thousand. "*Ultimo*," he declared, waiting for a response.

I must have seemed indifferent, and I think my mood puzzled him. Perhaps he thought me disappointed in the exhibits.
Turning away, he gazed out the window. When we reached the

outskirts of Cremona, he turned back, made an effort to sound genial, said, "I'll tell you what. If you're really a good violist..." He smiled broadly. "If I like the way you play, if I'm convinced you're the man you claim to be, I'll help you acquire the Mozart manuscript."

"It's a deal." I pulled myself together, shook hands. "And I think it's a great museum."

He dropped me off at the hotel, told me he looked forward to our little concert on Sunday morning. Much to my relief, The Destiny was still in the safe, and I carried it up to my room to practice. Istanbul, indeed!

11

Every morning, Franci knocked on my door, wheeled in a cart, served breakfast in my room. He would also bring up The Destiny from the safe in Luria's office, wipe the viola case with a clean towel before handing it to me.

The conference was over, the string players had checked out, and on Sunday, the hotel was quiet. After breakfast, I tuned the Voice of Manush, warmed up, went down to the music room, where Luria's wife, Sara, already sat at the piano, playing impeccable scales, a stout, pleasant woman with gray hair, dark eyebrows, and a serious face. Her fingers tossed arpeggios like gold coins, and she occupied the bench like a throne. Still a *virtuosa*.

The piano had been moved to the center, chairs and music stands arranged near it, and by the wall, more chairs lined up to hold an audience. Luria shook hands, patted my shoulder, greeted a few friends who drifted in to sit in the chairs. Salomone staggered in, leaning on his crutch. Luria introduced me to Odisseo Saggio, professor at the School of Musicology, who looked intently at The Destiny, tucked under my arm. "Exceptionally large viola," he observed, then searched my face, waiting for an explanation.

Luria interrupted, embracing his daughter, a younger reflection of her mother—plump, dark short hair, serious. "Here is *Dottoressa* Luria," he said, his arm around his daughter, smiling down at her, and introduced me. "*Dottore* Child claims to be a violist. We're going to test his credentials. He's also a heart specialist from Boston."

"From Boston," she said as we shook hands. "How nice. Do you know Roger Wilcox at Children's Hospital?"

"Not personally," I replied, then took a risk. "But I've heard him lecture."

"And Paul Dudley White. You must have known him."

"The Grand Old Man," I replied. "Everyone knew him. They say he carried a bicycle pump instead of a stethoscope, and that's almost true. He always commanded his people to keep fit. I did some of my residency under his supervision, but I think he taught me more about bicycles than cardiology."

"Charming," she said. "Ah, here's Isacco." A tall man with a high forehead, rimless spectacles, and a long jaw entered, carrying a cello. He leaned over, she stood on her toes and kissed him, laughing, "Darling, some day we'll stop meeting like this."

Luria explained, "Young people today are a study in perpetual motion. They commute to each other. Raquele is a pediatrician and she practices in Brescia. Isacco is a professor of law at the University of Florence. May I introduce my future son-in-law? *Dottore* Child, this is Isacco Lampronti."

I tried to remember our conversation in the library of Luria's establishment, when he read me the document on young Mozart. "The same name," I said, "the physician who's your ancestor. Morgagni's friend, the rabbi of Ferrara."

Luria beamed. "Exactly. Raquele and Isacco are distant cousins. Their marriage will reunite the two families."

Sara offered me a stack of piano quartet music, along with scores for string trios, in case we wanted to play while she dropped out. In my experience, four instruments are more work than three, and a trio is more fun. The fourth instrument—piano or extra violin—changes the chemistry, makes a quartet more demanding.

It was certainly not the first time I had played with strangers, but the little audience made it feel like a concert, while I had expected an informal social occasion, a chance to get acquainted. To warm up, we plunged into a reduction of the third Brandenburg, with Sara playing the continuo part. I played as if the Voice of Manush were an ordinary viola, felt odd warming up, tried to sense their level of skill and sensibility. Being good players, they adjusted to my timbre and intonation, but Isacco sounded a little raspy, Raquele not as clear as I would have liked. They waited for me to select the first piece.

Since I was being tested, I thought I would challenge them as well, and chose the Brahms quartet in C minor, Opus 60, his last piano quartet. A difficult piece, but I wanted to explore the range of Manush in an ensemble. And I chose it with Sara in mind as well. Anything by Brahms involving the piano challenges the pianist more than the string players. I'd give them a run for their money.

The piano opened with a single chord, and the strings offered a somber response. *Yaah-da. Yaah-da.* The piano challenged us with another chord. Deep and dark, the opening section demanded warm, beautiful sound from the strings. Then we slogged through a long dull line with a boring sostenuto. In that rhythmic interplay of violin, viola, cello, you have to feel the pulse in the long note. The jagged, restless first movement was a dense tangle of half-formed statements with haunting moments of repose.

Finishing together, we looked at one another with surprise. The second movement was as restless and craggy as the first, a rush of tragic cries from the abyss, ending in questions. *What now? Where to?* No relief until the third movement, a moving elegy introduced by sublime melody on the cello. An unforgettable song of the soul, repeated sweetly on the violin.

In the last movement, Sara did a fine job in the finale, her piano articulating the dense structure of interlocking melodies, bringing the work to a close with stately affirmation. She still performed as if she were a concert artist, but the Brahms was tough, and she needed to rest. Patting her forehead with a kerchief, she told us to go on without her.

I picked out a trio by Mozart. In an entirely different mood, we started the E-flat Divertimento, the only string trio Mozart completed, a complex work of many emotions, and in my opinion the finest trio in the string literature. In the first Allegro, we rushed through a difficult passage which threw us off stride. Cello made his entrance a beat and a half late, causing violin to hesitate and me to lose track of where we were. We floundered for a few measures, recovered, finished together. Raquele laid her violin on the carpet, looked at me out of the corner of her eye and said, "We sound like atrial fibrillation."

I sensed she was testing me and snapped back cheerfully, "Not that irregular. We had some rhythm going, even though it was ragged."

She seemed content with my reply, but thought for a moment and said, "Doctor, I'm so glad to have you here, so I can ask your advice. I have a little patient with ventricular septal defect and Eisenmenger syndrome. Do you think it's time to consult a surgeon?" No doubt this time—an open challenge. Nothing subtle about it. She looks like her mother but acts like her father, I thought.

"Hell, yes!" I said. "Not a moment to lose—but when it gets that far, it's probably inoperable." She had described an advanced stage of congenital heart disease.

"Of course," she replied, and picked up her fiddle. We both grinned. Her smile said, "You pass."

We resumed the Divertimento and hurried through, performing only the three principal movements, skipped the two minuets and the Andante variations. I thought we played apologetically, feeling we abused the music by our lack of preparation.

After we stopped, Raquele and Isacco set aside their instruments, but I wanted to test the Voice of Manush on an audience. Lowering the tuning, I played the cello part from the Brahms Andante movement, the sweet song of the soul. Isacco looked surprised. Then I raised the tuning to the violin range and gave them as much of *The Lark* as I could play.

Silence. As if they refused to acknowledge what they heard.

Salomone burst out, "*Bravo! Bravissimo*, maestro! Perhaps you've all lost your tongues, but surely you still have ears. This man is no *dottore*." I felt a tremor of anxiety. Was the old man calling my bluff? "*Squisito!* From now on we call him *maestro*."

"*Veramente!*" Luria agreed.

The praise supported my mood of elation, almost invincibility. Exalted by the music, absorbed in The Destiny, I could do anything I willed. Nothing could go wrong. Russell was absurd to think I might carry the Voice of Manush to Istanbul. The secret of life was vibrating in my hands. I refused to give it up.

Professor Saggio shook my hand warmly. "*Bellissimo!*" he said, asked to see the Voice, turned it over in his hands, squinted into the sound holes. "A remarkable instrument. Did you know Mozart worked on another string trio before he wrote the one you performed? Not the fragment in G major, but one that's never been published, an unusual piece for violin, cello, and something he called *tremegisto*, a large fiddle with three voices. Must have been a viola like yours. Come visit me at the Scuola. I teach in the morning, but afternoon is a good time to discuss. Come late any afternoon and I'll show you the manuscript." He thanked Luria for inviting him and left.

12

Luria grasped my shoulders and said, "Maestro Child! You conquer my skepticism. *Credo! Credo! Lo credo bene!* I believe you are indeed a violist as well as a doctor. Tomorrow I have to be in Milan, but come to my office Tuesday morning and we'll conspire to get the Mozart manuscript." I said nothing about my conversation with Saggio, who sounded so well-disposed toward me, perhaps I didn't need Luria's help.

Monday afternoon, I phoned Gerry at the library to report the manuscript was virtually in my pocket, asked her to confirm a price. I told her I wanted to stay in Europe a little longer, but felt uneasy about carrying around a valuable manuscript. In the back of my mind, Russell's challenge to my ownership of The Destiny troubled me, and I intended to do something about it, even if it were no more than a symbolic gesture. I made plans to return to England and ask Kate to document my title.

Gerry replied that if I wanted to stay longer it was no problem. She would send Lark, the keeper of manuscripts, as a courier to pick it up. "And Harold," she said warmly before I hung up the phone, "we miss you."

To visit Saggio, I walked across town on the Via Dante to Corso Garibaldi, carrying the Voice in its viola case, and found the Palazzo dell'Arte, a magnificent granite building which housed several schools. Inside, to the right of the courtyard, I wandered into the International School of Violin Making, intending to see their museum before I called on Saggio.

On a folding chair in the chill stone lobby, like a radiant jewel on dull gray flagstones, sat one of the most beautiful women I ever saw. She was about nineteen, with exquisite north-Italian features, her blonde hair drawn back in a short ponytail. She wore a light-blue corduroy shirt, jeans, sneakers, gold earrings, a bright scarf around her throat, and held a violin case on her lap. She returned my stare with an amiable smile. Perhaps my viola case reassured her. If I played a string instrument, I couldn't be all bad. "*Buongiorno*," she said with a little laugh.

I explained I was a visitor from America, wanted to look around the school and see the museum. Was she waiting for a violin lesson? I asked. She replied all the students were required to study violin. I was amused because she violated my stereotype of what an artisan should look like, yet felt amazed this beauty should be a student luthier. I expected her to be a model or a movie star.

"Do you enjoy playing the fiddle?" I asked, casting about for material to prolong the conversation.

"I don't mind playing," she replied. "I'm adequate, not gifted. But I love shaping wood. Would you like to go up and see the *ragazzi* working at their benches?"

Of course. I would have followed her anywhere. Halfway up the stairs we were halted by a roar from below. The custodian, a fierce old woman with a cane, shouted it was not allowed for visitors to go upstairs. We descended, the young woman smiling apologetically. At that moment, a dark good-looking young man came down a few steps, and my heart sank. Her teacher. If she's not his lover, this guy's got a problem, I thought. How in the world does he keep his mind on the music? She waved at me and went up to him, left me with the custodian who leaned on her stick and glared.

I let her show me into the museum, around the corner on the ground floor, and I spent ten minutes looking at the exhibits, no Stradivari things at all, but mostly the work of people associated with the school. Outside again, I asked directions to the Scuola di Paleografia e Filologia Musicale—the School of Musicology where Saggio worked. Across the courtyard, upstairs.

The young woman's image stayed in my mind. The first woman to stir me since I left Boston. Would I see her again? My feelings about her led me back to Russell's warning. Was she the one? How could I tell a woman whose name I didn't even know to see her gynecologist?

13

When I asked for Professor Saggio, they told me to wait in the Biblioteca. I browsed in the catalogue, an archaic system of handwritten volumes that stood upright on oak tables.

Greeting me warmly, Saggio led me to his office, pointed to a chair. I sat opposite him, looking through a narrow opening in a pile of books and papers on his desk. His head was bald except for a fringe around the back, but the lower half of his face grew an exuberant black curly beard and mustache, as if to compensate for deprivation above. A dark cigar sent up a plume of smoke, like a signal out of a forest. I asked about his work. He taught musical paleography and served as keeper of manuscripts, but his real love was teaching the folklore of music.

He asked to see The Destiny and once again squinted through the sound holes at the label. "Very interesting," he exclaimed. "Experts will judge it's a fake because Stradivari's initials are surrounded by three rings one inside the other. An authentic Stradivari label has only two rings. But let me tell you something. Three rings, one inside the other, is the symbol of Hermes Trismegistus." Putting out his cigar, he said, "Come with me."

Carrying the Voice of Manush, I followed him down the hall to the treasure room of the Biblioteca, a room with a large oak table and chairs in the middle, a bank of metal cabinets, and glass cases around the edges, cases exhibiting books and manuscripts. Unlocking a metal cabinet, he drew out a cardboard box. "From the Asioli family," he said. "Papers of Karl Thomas Mozart. Luria sold them to us last year." He opened a folder, showed me a letter from Constanze Mozart to her son. *More gems from my treasure chest, Karlchen. Bits and pieces your father never finished.*

Saggio's voice dropped to whisper, "Incomplete sketches." He handed me manuscripts in Mozart's own handwriting, sketches for *Thamos, King of Egypt*. "Some of this music went into the *Singspiel* named *Zaide*," Saggio explained. I saw page after page headed *Thamos, König in Aegypten*. "Look here!" Saggio whispered. From the middle he extricated a few sheets of music with a different heading, *Hermes in Aegypten*. "Unpublished, uncatalogued, unknown," Saggio observed, "never even noticed by either Köchel or Einstein. Why? Because they never saw these manuscripts, and even if they had seen them, this one is buried in the Thamos music. No one dreamed Wolfgang Amadeus Mozart wrote a different piece called *Hermes in Egypt*. He never mentioned it to his father, never mentioned it in any letter that survived. And see how it's scored. E-flat major, a trio for violin, cello, and tremegisto." His eyebrows shot up. "What the hell is a *tremegisto?* Maybe you hold the answer." He looked down at my viola case.

"How much is the manuscript worth?" I asked. "How much will you sell it for?"

"That's up to my board of governors, but as far as I'm concerned it's *impensabile*. This manuscript is not for sale." We examined the score together. "Would you like to have a copy?" he asked. "Why not? You should play it some day. The piece is written for your instrument. I'll make a copy on the machine."

Should I try to bargain? Tell him now the library wanted to buy the original and might offer a good price for it? Or wait till Lark arrived with the money? I decided to wait. After all, my purpose was to find the music and play it on The Destiny. I didn't owe anything to the Amy Beach Music Library. I didn't have to stay involved.

We pondered the music, a solitary movement in sonata form. Was it part of some larger structure? The so-called *tremegisto* was scored in the viola range, unless it rose to double the violin, or dropped to accompany the cello. The key changed from E-flat to C minor to C major, modulations reserved for Mozart's most profound religious and Masonic music. Three keys with important musical and philosophical relations, Saggio observed: E-flat, with its three flats in the key signature, represented Hermes Trismegistus. Its relative minor, C minor, stood for darkness and suffering, while its parallel major, C major, was the key of light, the triumph of good over evil. Saggio pointed out familiar themes in the music, ideas that went into the E-flat Symphony, *The Magic Flute*, and the

Jupiter. "You need to organize a trio and play this," Saggio urged, handing me the photocopies. "Take it with the blessing of Mozart." He chuckled. "And Hermes as well."

Once again in his office, with a photocopy of the score in my viola case, I puffed on the cigar he offered, sat back in the chair. As he lit a fresh cigar for himself and we puffed in harmony, as the room filled with smoke, he told me about Mozart's *Hermes in Egypt*. "You know anything about Hermes Trismegistus?" he asked.

"I certainly do," I replied. Without pausing to ask exactly what I knew, he plunged into his story.

Several years before, Saggio took a leave from his teaching post to work on an advanced degree and study musicology in Paris. He was determined to master paleography because there were difficult old manuscripts in the collection at the Scuola waiting to be read, but for his thesis, he chose to investigate Mozart in Paris, to explore his musical environment in 1778, because it was a turning point in Mozart's creative life, his graduation to maturity.

Everything written about Mozart's six months and three days in Paris left Saggio feeling skeptical and restless. Mozart and his mother arrived in March, she died in July, he departed alone in September, despising the frivolous, corrupt world of French aristocracy. The visit was a failure, the books said. Paris was a dismal, tragic experience for Mozart: visiting great houses, courting princes, duchesses, and counts, seeking commissions and students, hoping for a patron, suffering humiliation at every turn. The wealthy don't know what friendship means, Mozart wrote in one of his letters.

Despite depression over his financial prospects and grief

over the death of his mother, Mozart composed in Paris, completed violin sonatas started earlier, wrote choral works, arias, flute concerti, the sinfonia concertante for winds, the oboe concerto, piano sonatas, and two symphonies (one of which is lost).

Feeling there was a lot more to Mozart's experience in Paris than met the eye, Saggio traced the records of Mozart's friends, searched the huge eighteenth-century manuscript collection of the Bibliothèque National for diaries and letters. From these manuscripts, Saggio gathered a different story of Mozart in Paris, more complex than the traditional picture.

Saggio rested his cigar in an ashtray, moved his chair around the desk till we sat knee to knee, leaned over, spoke in a soft, low voice, speaking of Mozart's life with a certain delicacy, hesitating here and there, as if confiding intimate details about his best friend. He clasped his hands, looked at me speculatively, as if he were taking a risk, as if he wondered, could I be trusted with this information? Another fanatic, I thought.

According to Saggio, Mozart played viola in a quartet that included Count August von Hartzfeld, a young Hungarian nobleman whose Magyar name was Zsombolya. Hartzfeld was a fine violinist who loved Gypsy music. He knew all the Gypsy musicians in Paris. One fiddler intrigued Mozart, a Hungarian Gypsy named Rigo Manava, who had travelled all over Europe, and played on a huge viola he claimed was made for his father by Stradivari himself.

Saggio had plenty to say about Mozart, but that's not the point of this story. The main point is I came away from his office with the little experiment for strings—beautiful music Mozart composed for The Destiny.

14

I returned to the hotel for a moment, handing the instrument to Franci for deposit in Rossi's safe, then hurried to the Stradivari museum, peering at every scrap of paper, looking for some evidence to prove Stradivari had made The Destiny. I stood alone in the exhibit hall, and the guard watched me move from case to case. Finally, as I was about to leave, he approached me to say, "There's more in the back. *Rifiuti*. A drawer full of rubbish they never sorted out."

"Why didn't you tell me before?" I barked. "I've been in here several times."

The old man looked offended, and I regretted my outburst. He shrugged. "Didn't know what you wanted, *signore*. No one ever asks to see the rubbish."

He unlocked a door in the back leading to an alcove, pulled out a drawer which contained dozens of plastic boxes, let me open them. "These pieces are ambiguous, *signore*, and lack precise attribution. It's unknown if they belong to the master or his sons or possibly someone else."

About halfway through the boxes I found it—a trace, a sign, more than enough to feed the imagination. A large, folded scrap of light-brown paper with a drawing to mark positions for the upper and lower ends of the f-holes on a large viola. Across the top, someone had recorded in shaky handwriting: *Exact measurement for the sound holes of il Tremegisto made expressly for Mihaly the Gypsy.* He had drawn a line through two words, *la Trinità*, and written *il Tremegisto* above them.

When the guard led me out of the back room, I went to the exhibit cases again, hoping to find some trace I had missed. So preoccupied was I with The Destiny, trying to remember the voice of Papio Tamás reciting Minugia's tales of Mihaly in the Stradivari workshop, that I didn't hear Gerry Giraki come in, didn't see her until she stood at my elbow and said, "They told me I'd find you here."

She wore trim beige slacks with pointy-toed boots and a loose jacket, carried a soft leather shoulder bag, a silk scarf with gold flecks and ruby swirls flowing over the other shoulder. I was used to seeing her hair bound in a single long braid, but now it flowed round her shoulders. I stared at her dumbfounded, my gaze frozen in an endless split second, startled by the lovely face I knew so well yet could not identify because she was unexpected and out of place.

The recognition came in a rush of excitement, which unsettled me. I trembled inside. Would the distance between us, so difficult to keep in Boston, survive in Cremona? Now she reached out to be hugged, and I held her close. I could think of nothing to say but, "What are you doing here?"

"I came for a lark," she said. Peering into an exhibit case, she asked, "What are you doing here?"

I wondered, for a moment, how to explain. "I have a remarkable instrument..." I began.

She grinned, looked up at me, deep black eyes rimpling at the corners, and said, "I don't doubt it." Before I could recover my composure, she spied a cello at the back of the room, an instrument made by a student working in the manner of Stradivari. Rushing over to the exhibit case, she exclaimed, "Oooh, I want one of those!" After she looked over the instruments made by followers of Stradivari, we left the museum, strolled back to the hotel. She held my arm as we walked and hummed something in her rich contralto. "Like it?" she asked.

"I don't recognize the melody."

"That's because I just composed on the plane, thinking of being with you here. I call it *Souvenir of Cremona*—wrote it for a string sextet, like Tchaikovsky's *Souvenir of Florence*."

"It does remind me of that, now that you mention it."

"Because the pitch elements are the same as Tchaikovsky's, but I'm going to restructure his opening notes as a chord. I hope the resonances will remind people of his piece." I would have to tell her I didn't have the original Mozart manuscript after all. Why didn't she wait for a phone call?

When we sat at a table in the restaurant, she sighed and squeezed my hand. "So good to see you," she said. I ordered two cognacs and a bunch of grapes. We sipped, contemplating each other. Back at the library, her black hair, alert dark eyes, athletic build, made me think of Artemis, and since she ruled the orchestra, taming our wild sounds, I had called her

Mistress of the Beasts. But now the look in her eye made me think of Aphrodite. We're in Italy, I thought. Venus, not Aphrodite.

"Where are you staying?" I asked.

"Room 507. Nice big room..." She hesitated, and I sensed she almost said, *with a nice big bed.*

"Who's watching the store?"

"Nothing much going on," she replied. "I need a break."

"And you came for a lark?"

"Lark's afraid to be with you alone," she explained, a ripple of fun in the corners of her mouth. Was she pulling my leg? I couldn't be sure.

Forcing a smile, I said, "Doesn't seem like you're scared."

Forcing a smile to mimic me, she leaned forward, elbows on table, chin on the palms of her hands, said in a theatrical voice, "You're *so* perceptive."

"But I don't get it. She's a black belt in karate."

"It's not physical harm she's afraid of."

Sound jocose, I thought, make it funny. "You mean she's scared I'll get her in my power. Cast a spell?"

"You *are* irresistible," Gerry teased.

"Those damn rumors."

"Here's a new one that will amuse you, Harold. They say you're really impotent, and all the rumors you're a mighty stud are just to cover up."

I ordered two more cognacs. The cool side of my head pondered her motivation. Bored with her job and out to have some fun? Just flirting? Wanting to test the rumors and confirm one or the other? Or maybe—just possibly—she liked me? Yearning to respond to her warmth, I felt chilled by thinking of the seed of death inside her. I slid the bunch of grapes on the table between us. "With all those rumors," I said, "we couldn't expect a lark to rendezvous with a predatory bird like me. But why did you take her place?"

She looked into my eyes so straight and deep, it made me shiver. "In Greek, Giraki means *falcon*," she said.

"Then we're birds of a feather," I replied.

When the waiter brought our cognacs, she fluttered her fingers over my glass, as if she were dropping a powder into it. "Magic potion," she said.

"To make me potent?"

"To make you dream."

That gave me an opening. "I do dream, Gerry. Prophetic dreams. That's how I know what I'm about to tell you."

Another waiter, the skinny one with light-blue eyes, who had asked Franci if I were a magician, appeared at my elbow, whispered in my ear, "*Dottore* Child, you must come at once. It's urgent!" I told him not to interrupt—I would go as soon as possible.

"Gerry," I said, finding it difficult to say the right words, "I like you a lot."

"I was hoping." She smiled, rubbed the back of her neck.

"When's the last time you had a medical examination?"

She looked stunned, hurt crossing her face to make way for disbelief. "You son of a bitch," she whispered.

"Gerry, please don't misunderstand me." The skinny waiter with light-blue eyes stood behind her at the doorway, gesturing for me to come away. I scowled, but he persisted. Something was up. I would have to talk fast. "Soon after you get home, you'll think you're pregnant." The look on her face turned cold and cautious, the look of someone who suspected she was talking to a madman. "But you're not pregnant. It's a real bad cancer. The doctor will know what to do."

The skinny waiter looked determined, moved in my direction. "Emergency," I said. "Please wait for me, Gerry, I'll be right back. I can explain everything."

I hurried out to the lobby. "It's Signor Rossi," the waiter said. "His heart is burst."

A crowd gathered outside the office. Rossi lay on the carpet, looking gray and cold. Someone had removed his tie, opened his collar. Rossi collapsed when he discovered my instrument was gone. Nothing else was missing from the safe. "Franci shattered his heart," the waiter said.

From the threshold, I heard the voice of Russell Flambard, speaking impeccable Cremonese. *Scusi, per favore, mi scusi.* The bloated apparition of Russell kneeled down by my side, set his black bag on the carpet. For my benefit he stank like a graveyard, revealed a belly full of worms. His hand on Rossi's forehead, he said to me, "With your permission, I'll take care of him."

15

Both Franci and Stella were gone. The clerk at the desk handed me an envelope which contained a sheet of hotel stationery with a few lines of neat penmanship. *Dear Signor Mago. I am sorry, but this is the only way to make you come to Murgia. My father is dying and you can save him. Your violino is under his bed. I wait at noon each day behind the bishop's back.*

Suppressing the impulse to run after Franci immediately, I stayed around, watched the undertaker carry Rossi away, spoke to Luria on the phone, talked to people, tried to learn about Murgia and the Lairone family. Little MOORRjah, they said, rolling the R—the heart of legendary Buca. "They're all pagans down there," the desk clerk said, "and brigands as well." No one else had much to offer, and I went up to pack my things. Gerry had not checked out, but I could not find her anywhere. I left a message in her box, explaining my intention to go to

Murgia, described my itinerary.

That night, I dreamed Gerry was in my room, lying on the bed naked, slowly growing smaller. My viola case was pink, shaped like a woman's body with breasts and a subtle mound of Venus. I opened the case and drew out the Voice of Manush to play in the hallway. Shrinking smaller and smaller, Gerry crawled into the case. I shut it, locking her inside, went into the hall and played. When I returned to the room, the viola case was gone. I searched all over and wept, tormented by an intense feeling of desolation.

In the morning, feeling terrible, I skipped breakfast, left the hotel, learning Gerry had already checked out. I drove to Milan in a rented car, flew to Brindisi, rented a car again, headed up the coast of rocky Puglia.

Murgia was about twenty-five miles northwest of Brindisi and seven miles inland from the cove local people still refer to as Cala San Diomedo. The highway ran through vineyards, olive groves, orchards of almond trees. Spring had come early, and the countryside looked green, here and there speckled with gray trulli shelters. This was trulli country, full of corbelled stone buildings with conical roofs. Trullo builders erected them without mortar by laying courses of expertly placed stones, each one projecting over the stone below. The form of the building resembled a prehistoric beehive-shaped tomb, and trulli were originally built to fool the stupid tarantulas. According to local superstition, death spiders on the prowl, thinking everyone inside a trullo was already dead, might pass it by. In Murgia, I heard, most people dwelt in concrete houses, but some folk still lived in manmade caves as well as trulli.

After Ostuni, halfway to Cisternino on a road that followed

the old mule track, I reached Murgia, the little town at the foot of Monte La Morte.

Once again, I read Franci's note. Behind the bishop's back, it said. On the edge of Murgia, I stopped at a café to ask where I might find the bishop. The woman looked puzzled, informed me there was a big cathedral in Brindisi, a smaller one in Monopoli. Which bishop did I want? Then where might I find the Lairones? Try the petrol station, she suggested, the one on Via Rosmini in the west side of town.

All along the way I had noticed only a chain of automatic gas pumps, where you never see a human attendant, but put your money into a metal slot. The AGIP logo on these stations displayed the left side of a dragon, more like a black dog, looking over its shoulder, breathing red fire over its tail. But here was an old-fashioned service station with a grease rack and garage. Lairone's Petrol Station. The sign in front showed a green and black heron.

I asked for a lube job and oil change, although I was driving a brand new rental Ford which didn't need a thing. The grease rack was not the kind that goes way up, the kind you walk under, but a short hydraulic lift which raised it a few feet, and the mechanic stood in a rectangular grease pit below. The man I spoke to had a big mustache, black patch over one eye, a gold earring, red kerchief over his hair—the child's stereotype of a pirate. I asked for Francesco Lairone. Two men in black coveralls suddenly appeared, stood behind him.

"Haven't seen Franci in years," the pirate replied in thick Murgiese. "He and his sister work up north."

I asked to use the toilet and when I returned, the pirate was on his knees looking up under the car. He gestured to me in an agitated manner. "Look here!" he shouted. When I hesitated, he said, "You're in mortal danger, *signore*." I crouched, looking up under the car, and he shoved me over the edge of the pit. Two men caught me as I fell, twisted my arms behind, and as a door opened in the side of the grease pit, carried me into a dark room. The pirate jumped down into the pit, closed the door, and they pinned me to the ground. I lay in total darkness, feeling the point of a blade in the side of my neck. The place smelled of grease and rubber. I should never have made the decision to pursue The Destiny on St. Swithin's Day. Is this where my life would end—in a vile and nasty place? Would they bury me near the grease pit under a pile of used tires?

16

A voice said in Murgiese, "Slit his throat!"

"Who is he?"

"A government weasel poking his nose into our burrow."

"Are you sure?"

"These stupid agents always drive Fords."

I had never felt so helpless. With just a glimmer of light I could have shifted into a tiger or a snake or anything to get out of there, but in the dark I had no power to change shape or distort their perceptions. Was this the end? I expected Russell to appear any moment to say I ran out of gas and congratulate me on a well-oiled finish. But I must have received help from somewhere, because my mind opened up, and I heard Papio Tamás in his merry storyteller voice recalling Minugia and Professor Raimondi, remembered the passwords of the secret society. Gasping, with a throat choked by mucus, I tried to speak. "Cousin! *Sono buono cugino*," I said.

"*Bugiardo!*" someone roared. "Fucking liar!"

"I'm your kinsman," I insisted.

"Wait!" another voice commanded. I felt the knife withdraw from my throat. Hands grabbed my arms, pulled me upright. "They say the Charcoal-burners are dead."

Coughing, I replied, "So they say."

"Then where are the graves?"

"The Charcoal-burners are buried in our hearts."

"*Saluti buon cugino!*" They embraced me, opened the door. "Forgive us, cousin, please." Shakily, I climbed a ladder out of the grease pit, followed them into a trullo behind the gas station.

We sat around a table, and a red-faced man who looked feverish poured cold *vino rosato* out of a pitcher. The pirate handed me a wet handkerchief to dab my bleeding neck, for the knife had pricked the skin. The third man, stocky and bald, had a white scar running across his forehead from temple to temple. Pirate followed my gaze as I wondered about the bald man's scar. "He had a bad headache, and Death poured him a set of new brains." Involuntarily, I looked at Pirate's eyepatch. "And I wear this thing to keep me from winking at the girls."

I heard their names, but in my mind they remained Pirate, Fever, and Headache. Pirate and Fever spoke in Murgiese dialect, but Headache rarely uttered a word. I was getting used to Murgiese, which made unusual changes in pronunciation, such as substituting *d* for *l*. Instead of *trulli*, for example, they said *truddi*. Fever warned me, "If you're lying to us, we'll kill you."

I replied, "My grandfather's godfather, Minugia, was the student of Umberto Raimondi when he lived in exile more than a century ago," and fishing in my pocket, handed him the gold disc with the head of Diomedes on one side, a heron on the other. He examined it, held the coin in his fist over his heart, and said in a low voice, "*Santo Diomedo.*" When he passed it to the others, they in turn did the same thing, held the coin over the heart, whispered "*Santo Diomedo.*"

They laid the coin on a white kerchief in the middle of the table. "Payment for your life," Pirate said.

"I felt close to death," I confessed.

"All of us in this room are close to Death," Pirate replied.

It struck me then with the force of lightning that nothing in my life was a coincidence, not my adoption, not my foster grandfather's stories, not my magic, not my apprenticeship on Fluaria, not my wandering life, not the Cambridge Sinfonia, not my chasing after The Destiny, not my presence in that room. In that flash, I recognized my weird. "Are you playmates of Death?" I asked.

"That's an American term. Frivolous. This is not a play-ground but a school, *una scuola di perfezionamento.*"

Not bad, I thought. That meant finishing school. A place for people who ran out of gas. "And here's our teacher," Fever said.

An old man, bent-over, leaning on a stick, and a slim old woman with thin wrists entered the room. Pirate introduced them as Umberto Raimondi and his wife, Giuseppina. He introduced me as the grandson of the godson of the student of Umberto Raimondi. One look at my bloody collar and she scowled. "Butchers!" she hissed at them, then said to me, "Give me that shirt. I'll return it to you in the morning."

I fetched my bag from the car, changed all my clothes, soiled by the floor of the room behind the grease pit, handed the bloodstained shirt to her. I felt uncomfortable doing it, but decided to go with the flow, and it was clear I was expected to stay overnight. There was no point in my running blindly after Franci. Better to stay cool and learn where his family lived. Another woman came in, tall, large-boned, silent, with long stringy hair. She was never introduced to me, and Raimondi's wife followed her into the kitchen.

When all the men were seated and drinking wine, Pirate waved his hand at the coin in the middle of the table. Raimondi picked it up, looked at both sides, said thank you, put it in his vest pocket. "Is your name really Umberto Raimondi?" I asked the old man.

He had spoken to the men in Murgiese, but now addressed me in pure, elegant Italian, the kind you hear around Florence and Siena. "The one you know about—the Raimondi who died in Paris—was the grandfather of my grandfather. I lived up north many years but came back here to die." He sighed, added bitterly, "If we ever get permission to die. Death has a way of neglecting his friends."

"Perhaps he wants you to live?" I offered.

"For reasons I don't understand. Destiny rules and Death obeys, but Music governs Destiny."

"I remember that," I said. "It's in the *Sayings of Hermes Trismegistus.*"

"Of course. But Death is overworked these days. As the death rate declines, population expands, and the absolute number of deaths goes up. Too much for angels or sphinxes or spiders to handle. More than fifty million humans die every year.

138,208 a day. Ninety-six each minute. Do you realize our friend must be in ninety-six different places every minute? But tell me about yourself. What do you need to learn? Why am I here?"

Instinct warned me to be cautious about my pursuit of Franci, since I didn't know if they were protecting him. I said I wanted to learn about Murgia, and wondered why Raimondi came back to this town. "I belong here," he replied sadly.

I said he seemed fluent in Murgiese, yet spoke beautiful Italian.

"Our local language is barely Italian," he observed. "People from other regions don't understand us. We sound like Greeks. But language is a clue to something else. We have a different spiritual constitution. The old religion never died here. Christendom, we say, ends at the Piazza."

Giuseppina brought in a basket of steaming hot bread and set the table. The tall silent woman followed with bowls of thick minestrone. I was hungry and gulped it down. "Why the Piazza?" I asked. "What Piazza?"

He soaked a piece of bread in minestrone, licked his fingers. "Late in the seventeenth century, Bishop Leone Puzzo organized a gang of vigilantes to stamp out heresy. The Murgia Inquisition, they called it. Our ancestors took their religion underground. The bishop claimed he triumphed over paganism, and the Church erected a bronze statue of Bishop Puzzo. You'll see it in the middle of town, in the Piazza di Pietà. Eventually, a death spider got the bishop. He came down with tarantism, refused to dance, and died of the spider bite, but he still divides us. Our people—half the population of this town—live on the other side of the Piazza, behind the bishop's back."

That's what the note meant! Behind the bishop's statue. Look for Franci there.

"It's a spiritual location too," he continued. "Everyone who venerates the Bones of Diomedes worships behind the bishop's back. Believe me, my friend, Murgia is a state of mind. In ancient times, it was in Daunia. A mystical country, Daunia, the Avalon of Italy, still alive in the imaginations of Pugliesi. Do you know our folklore? We tell our children the adventures of Diomedes, just as Greeks preserved the story of Odysseus and the tragedy of Oedipus. We claim descent from the companions of Diomedes, who turned into herons. In our hearts, Diomedes is still the King of Daunia."

Cautiously, I asked about Franci's family. "I understand his father is ill. Where does he live?"

"Can't miss it," he replied. Fedele Lairone was king of the trulli and lived down by the canyon they called Gravina Dolorosa. And did I know about the tragic division in the Lairone family? *Terribile!* Most awful thing you can imagine. Around the turn of the century, two ancestors, twin brothers, different as night and day, had a falling out. In those days, all the Lairones dwelt in caves, keeping the tradition of the founder, Diomedes. They lived on the other side of the Gravina Dolorosa. After the fatal quarrel, they divided the Bones of Diomedes in two caskets, and half the family followed one of the twin brothers, built trulli on the other side of the gorge.

"Now Lairones dwell all over the west part of town, but there's still a row of trulli on the edge of the Gravina facing the caves, and the senseless feud goes on. Away from the Gravina, both parties observe a truce, the kids go to school together, the adults chat politely in the marketplace. But on both sides of the ravine, the fight goes on. We in this room are Lairones of the trulli, and we still make war against Lairones of the caves. It's hell down there. The king of the caves is evil through and through. *Il Serpe*, the Snake, they call him, because he's full of venom. They say he spits *veleno*. He's a clever, deadly poisoner, ready to kill any Lairone from our side of the family. Both kings have the power of *malocchio*, the evil eye, and both of them are *gettatori*, they can throw it from a distance. They creep around the rocks on both sides of the Gravina, hoping to catch a glimpse of each other so they can throw the evil eye. It's like a battlefield. And very tough for Franci, who's in love with Rosa, the only daughter of the Snake."

After the minestrone, the women served us boiled *fave*, delicious mashed beans saturated in hot olive oil, with breaded zucchini, little tomatoes, and delicately bitter greens. I wanted to help them, but they were shocked by my offer, insisted I sit down and eat, not get in their way. When we almost finished, the two women sat down to eat with us. After the meal, Pirate handed round little glasses of *vino cotto*, a concentrated, aromatic wine.

I felt exhausted and slept well that night in a little room at the back of the trullo. In the morning, Pirate returned my shirt, which Giuseppina had washed and ironed. He served me hot bread and coffee, said I could leave my car there if I wanted to walk into town, invited me to return and stay another night.

17

Franci's note said he would wait at noon each day behind the bishop's back. I spent the morning wandering around town, and a little before twelve, headed for the Piazza Pietà. The bishop faced the Christian part of Murgia, standing in cope and miter, crosier in the left hand, two fingers of his right hand elevated to bless the east. Russell Flambard sat on the steps of the pedestal behind the bishop's back.

"Where's Franci?" I asked.

"In hospital, I should be there now. Poor chap is lingering."

Knowing better than to ask questions, I followed him up Via Agnus Dei, walking swiftly. For a fat man, Russell moved fast. The Ospedale Civile was in Garibaldi Square, and in less than ten minutes we were there. "Consulting physicians," Russell told them at the desk. The lift moved up very slowly. Fourth floor. I went into the room, while Russell lingered in the hall.

Stella, two young men, and a white-haired woman were at his bedside. Franci looked greenish gray, wasted, an intravenous system plugged into his arm, tubes connecting him to bottles on the floor. A young doctor, northern Italian, with brown hair, blue eyes, golden beard, was writing on the chart. He glanced alertly at me through wire-rimmed spectacles, and I sensed a man of the highest intelligence. Franci groaned, said, "At last. *Dottore* Child."

The doctor looked relieved, said quickly, "You're his physician?"

Franci said, "Yes, yes. He will heal me."

I wondered what to say. The doctor took my elbow, led me out of the room, introduced himself, "Enrico Alghisi."

"Harold Child," I replied.

"He's not going to make it," the doctor said. "Serious dehydration, electrolyte imbalance. Nausea, diarrhea, severe cramps, convulsions."

"Bacterial infection?" I asked.

"You're not Italian," he observed.

"From Boston," I replied, "but I've just come down from Cremona."

"I'm from Firenze," he confided, "and wish to hell I were back there. Chose to do my residency in Murgia because I wanted to study the local folk medicine. But I'm just fiddling in Buca." That was a regional expression. Pugliesi would say about anyone who actively engaged in superstitious practices, he or she was *fiddling in Buca*. "Facilities in this town are beyond belief," he continued. "They have one toxicologist, who gets mortally ill with food poisoning, his assistant is incompetent, and I can't get clear results from a blood test. I have to go into the lab and do it myself."

"What's your diagnosis."

"Ricin. But I can't be sure."

I scratched my head. "Is that a disease?"

"A poison. He's going to die. Family says it's murder."

"What the hell is ricin?" I asked.

"Comes from the castor oil plant. It's like arsenic, produces symptoms easy to mistake for an infection, inflames the intestinal tract, splits red cells so they can't bring oxygen to brain and heart. But it's the electrolytic imbalance that will kill him." He handed me the chart, squeezed my arm. "I'll be right back. Just want to run down to the lab."

I went back into the room, laid the chart at the foot of the bed. Franci said, "Signor Mago, my father is dying. After you heal me, take care of him. Your *violino* is under his bed."

The door opened and Russell entered, wearing a white coat, carrying a black bag. Scowling at me, he said in English, "Don't get ideas! He's mine." To the others, he spoke in flawless Murgiese. "Everybody out for five minutes please. I'll take care of him now."

18

In the hallway they told me what happened to Franci. He had been in love with Rosa since they went to school together, but she never returned his love and he left town to work far away in Cremona. The very day Franci came back to Murgia, the Snake—Rosa's father—spotted him in the marketplace, acted friendly, said it was time for the senseless feud to end, invited Franci to walk home with him to the cave. He gave him a glass of wine, and that night, back in the family trullo, Franci collapsed with dreadful pains in his abdomen.

Despite the feud, bad news always travelled fast across the Gravina. Rosa collapsed as well. Don't misunderstand, this was no Romeo and Juliet story. Rosa didn't love Franci and probably helped her father entice Franci into the cave, but something went wrong and she drank some of the wine her father prepared for Franci. A few people said the Snake for some unknown reason deliberately poisoned his daughter, which is absurd. She probably didn't know the wine was poisoned, and maybe she drank out of the beaker when her father was out of the room or even after Franci left the cave. The truth is we don't know how or when she drank it. The romantics in the trulli community say she did it deliberately, because in secret, against the will of her father, she really did love Franci.

Russell was gone when we went back into the hospital room, and I stood by uncomfortably as they wept over Franci's corpse. I tried to comfort them when the attendant removed him to the hospital morgue. With mixed feelings, I walked back to the trullo with Stella, Franci's mother, and his two brothers, felt excited in the midst of all that grief because I was getting closer to The Destiny.

The family occupied the largest trullo in the row facing the Gravina. The roof displayed a heron whitewashed on the stones and a tall ornamental pinnacle with a ball on top capped the conical dome. From the doorway, I could see the enemy dwellings across the canyon, cave houses dug into the cliff of soft volcanic rock. Below the cave houses, steps carved into the rock, stairs with prominent handholds beside them, led down into the gorge from both edges, but a hundred yards away, a narrow bridge of wood and steel poles crossed the ravine.

The late-afternoon sun, shining through the open door on the whitewashed walls, made the trullo bright inside. They led me to a bedroom, where Franci's father, king of the trulli, lay propped up on pillows. As soon as he saw their faces, he began to weep. I don't know how long I stayed in that room with them, some of me experiencing their grief, most of me eager to reach under the bed for the Voice of Manush. Eventually, after they served coffee and we shared memories of Franci, his father turned to me and said, "Heal me, mago, so I can kill the Snake."

"I need my fiddle," I replied and fished for the viola case under the bed. He was a robust man in his fifties, and when I examined him, could find nothing physically wrong.

"*Fascino,*" he insisted, meaning he was a victim of the evil eye. I thought it was an obvious case of delusional hysteria and doubted if the evil eye had touched him. I had once seen a man hit by a *gettatore,* witnessed the effects of *malocchio.* Instant fulguration, causing massive distortion in the electro-magnetic system of the body. But if I was correct about hysteria, hypnotic suggestion might be the cure.

"My fiddle has power over *malocchio.*" I began to play the local tarantella, *Leaping in Buca.* "My spell will break the *fascino.*" The Destiny quivered in my hands as I played. In twenty minutes, Franci's father was up and walking around, flexing his muscles, praising me as the greatest *mago* on earth. Then he collapsed in a chair, head in hands, weeping. I left them to their grief, carried the Voice outside.

By the bridge, in front of the little community of troglodytes, stood a large man with a huge mustache, watching me. From across the ravine, I could see the flame of his eyes. He gestured and I hesitated, but impelled by curiosity, I crossed the bridge. In the cliff behind him, I saw neat cave houses with modern wood doors, clotheslines, rain gutters and drip channels carved above the chimney holes. "Please, *mago,* heal my daughter. The doctor from Brindisi is with her now, but come in. I beg of you, heal my Rosa."

He turned around as Russell emerged from a door, carrying his black bag. Russell ignored the Snake, who started to speak, reached out his hands, looked perplexed, and stammered, "*Dottore...*"

Brushing past, Russell muttered to me, "I don't want you in that room. Get out of here. Fast!"

Following Russell across the bridge, I heard the Snake make choking sounds, call out, "*Dottore! Mago!* Please!"

19

That evening, after dinner in the trullo behind the petrol station, a crowd gathered in the little building. I heard rumors, conjectures, wise cracks.

"His fiddle has power to raise the dead."

"Too bad we have no tarantulas this year."

"Damn shame he didn't come a few years ago."

I should have known better, but I needed to play. The Destiny *made* me play. It's not correct to say I possessed the Voice again. Truth is it possessed me. The more I played, the more I wanted to hear its haunting resonance, exquisite sonority, feel its power to stir the heart. I felt inside me a lust to perform, a hunger as strong as sex. People standing in the doorway shouted, "Come outside!"

We stood in the gravelled yard before the trullo, with a crowd extending to the pumps of the petrol station. One after another I played traditional dances. "Umberto!" they shouted. "Where's Umberto?"

"Too old," croaked the old man, standing by my side.

"Don't worry about it!" someone replied. "His fiddle can raise the dead." I played a Murgiese saltarello.

"*Corragio*, Umberto!"

The old man straightened up, threw aside his walking stick, snapped his fingers. In the gravelled yard before the trullo, the old man danced. "Salta! Salta!" The crowd clapped, whistled, cheered. He didn't go far up in the air, always kept a foot on the ground, moved slowly, but he danced. Scowling, smiling, arms stretched wide, fingers snapping, head thrown back, eyes flashing, he danced. Next, I played once again the local tarantella, *Leaping in Buca*. He danced. Until Giuseppina cried out, "Enough, enough," and handed him her kerchief.

Sudden quiet. A burly man with a huge mustache pushed through the crowd. Ignoring them all, the Snake came up to me, talked as if we were alone. "You play like Paganini, *mago*," he uttered, as if expressing the most sorrowful message in the world.

"Nobody plays like Paganini," I replied.

"I know what you got there. I play fiddle sometimes."

"Thank you."

"Do one little thing for me, *mago*, I beg you. I kiss your hands." Ignoring the crowd, he fell on his knees.

Sensing grief might burst his chest, I decided to help him, loosened the bowstring, settled The Destiny into the viola case. "What can I do?"

"Come and play a requiem over my Rosa."

People in the crowd shrank back, made a path for us. I followed him across the bridge, but refused to go into the house, stood outside the threshold and played. Be cautious, I thought, but I needed to hear the music echo against the cliff, needed to hear the Voice of Manush on this side of the Gravina, singing about death. First I played the haunting *Lament for a Rose* by a student of Elgar whose name escapes me, a melody inspired by the lines of John Masefield:

Roses are beauty but I never see
Those blood drops from the burning heart of June
Glowing like thought upon the living tree
Without a pity that they die so soon.

Then I played Ravel's *Pavane for a Dead Princess*, left myself wide open, never expecting an attack. Absorbed in the music, I neglected the simplest precaution of sorcery. My inner gates were open, and I was defenseless.

When I glanced up, rage in the furnace of his eye shot to the core of my soul. Instant fulguration, rupturing the gate of life force between navel and spine. I felt excruciating pain explode in the pit of my gut, radiate through my body. The dark storm swirled around me as energy flowed out of my heart. I cradled The Destiny in my arms, crumpled to the ground. Before I fell, he tore the Voice out of my grasp. I reeled back, tumbling to the edge of the ravine, grabbed a handhold carved in the rock. It slipped away from me, and I slid toward the abyss.

20

How could I have been so careless? One of the first things Ametra taught me was to close my vital centers and wrap them in light. A simple precaution. But I was wide open. His lightning ruptured the gate between navel and spine. I felt my energy draining away, thought I was finished. Harold Child faded away, and I lay there in my old body, Marko Manava. I don't know how long I stayed unconscious, but every now and then I revived a little and looked around for Death. Still nowhere to be seen.

After a long spell of darkness, I felt someone carry me as if I were a baby. Whoever it was laid me down on a floor, removed my clothes, and massaged my body, first the back, then the other side, expertly kneading the region of my solar plexus, then rubbed my face and scalp. The hands were hot. I felt one hand on my heart, the other on my belly. Energy poured into me. I was picked up again, dressed in a loose garment, and put to bed. It happened several times until at last I opened my eyes.

I was lying on my back on a straw mat, my head cradled on the lap of someone holding his hand on my head. The warmth of that hand flowed into my brain. I glanced up and for a moment thought I looked into a mirror. The face gazing down at me resembled my own, but without my scars and wrinkles. My eyes, my beak of a nose, my gaunt face and prominent cheekbones. The young man, who was about twenty, had long black hair which fell over his shoulders. As he looked down at me, I tried the Old Language, "Please touch. I'm quiet. Let's be here together."

He replied in flawless English. "It's all right, Father. You're getting better. You're going to be all right."

I didn't know what to say. "Who are you?" I asked.

"I'm Arundo, Father. I've been taking care of you. You're healing nicely." He picked me up in his arms, and tall as I am, carried me easily, set me on the bed, and covered me with a sheet. Sitting on the edge of the bed, stroking my head, he explained, "Mother knew what was happening and she brought you here so I could look after you."

"Where are we?"

"San Diomedo, in the Tremiti Islands."

"She brought me here?"

He nodded. "She says to tell you you're still a jackass—and you never learned a thing from her."

"But she said her child could never see the face of its father."

"That's right, but I'm no child. I'm all grown up."

"And you're the ruling spirit of this place?"

"Of the entire archipelago. Mostly rocks."

"I'll be damned."

Under his care, I felt the gate of vitality close. The rupture healed, and my energy built up again. We took walks together, and he started me swimming nude in the cold salt water. It was one of the happiest times of my life. I was getting to know my own son. "I'm surprised you speak English," I said.

"She insisted I learn your mother tongue," he replied.

"My mother tongue is Omaha."

"I don't know what that means."

"I'll tell you about my life."

"Yes, things she never mentioned. I want to hear. She did tell me you know how to heal."

"You're a great healer," I said.

"Chip off the old block."

"Did Death come for me? Did you wrangle?" He didn't know what I was talking about. One day when we were sitting in the sun after a swim, I asked, "Tell me how you like it. Your life here I mean."

"Fine. It's a lot of responsibility, but I can handle it. As a kid growing up in Fluaria I had fun most of the time, but there were tedious moments. You know how pompous they sound when the old ladies get together and preach about the Ancient and Everlasting Law of the Mothers. But here I'm my own boss. She never interferes." I sensed his energy reaching out and probing the contours of my mind. I let him in a little, and he seemed pleased with what he found. "You know," he said, "you're different from the way I pictured you."

"How am I different?"

"Well, I imagined you looked like a Greek fisherman. But

you look like me. And I sense you're a lot like me. But I can't reach your inner thoughts yet. Maybe you even think like me."

"Maybe I do."

"You know, I thought of you as a sourpuss. As a disapprover."

"Why?"

"When I was a teenager, she used to push me around. She would say, 'If your father were here, he would not tolerate that kind of behavior.'"

I know my mouth must have fallen open in amazement. "She told you that?"

"You know how kids are. She spoiled my fun sometimes. She kept lecturing me about the old days. She and my sisters and the old ladies—her friends from the other islands—they kept saying how lucky I was. In the old days, I would have been sacrificed. Nothing clean like slitting my throat or cutting my balls off—but boiling in a cauldron. She kept talking about the cauldron, saying that some day I would get the point."

"The pot of plenty. She's a subtle spirit, your mother."

"Too subtle for me. I think it's sick."

"The surface meaning is the goddess makes a stew out of her children. The profound, hidden meaning is her magic keeps them safe, and they derive power and wisdom from the cauldron. Let's be fair to your mother. That's what she meant."

"I'm glad you're here to explain it to me. And I'm just glad you're here."

"I'm glad too, and grateful you saved my life."

"I like taking care of you."

"And I can tell you enjoy living on this island. You're having a good time."

"It's a pretty good deal." He was probing my feelings again.

"The nymphs..." I started to say.

He looked at me cautiously, "They take a lot of time."

I smiled. "How are they?"

His face was like the sun coming out of a cloud. "They're terrific!"

We walked a lot, then sailed to another island. "Dad, about the nymphs. I can fix you up..."

I replied with a poker face, "When I was young, I had my fill."

"You did?"

"Enough to last a lifetime."

I lost track of the days and wanted to stay there forever, but one day he reminded me. "Dad—about the guy who clobbered you..." Unfinished business. The Snake. "I wouldn't let him get away with it," he said. I remained silent. He was right, I felt. And I must recover The Destiny. "If I were you, I mean," he added apologetically.

I stayed another week, and he sailed me to the mainland. I hugged him and stood on the dock, a duffel at my feet. "About your childhood..."

"Yes?"

"Do you have any regrets?"

"Not really. I'm happy to be me. Except..."

"Except what?"

"She taught me the flute and all—but I wish..."

"What?" I demanded.

"I wish I could play the fiddle."

I stood on the dock and watched him sail away, kept my eyes on him till the boat was a dot on the horizon.

21

By the time I returned to Murgia, the situation at the Gravina Dolorosa had changed. The war was over, and the factions had reunited the Bones of Diomedes in a single casket. Now Lairones mingled freely on both sides of the ravine, and the Snake lay dying in his cave. "He made a mistake in his *farmacia* and poisoned himself," Stella said. She led me across the bridge into his house, took me through the chambers, while people wandered in and out. The fortress was now a museum.

She showed me around the *farmacia*, a suite of linked chambers with cistern, channels, settling basins, drying benches carved in the rock. In the old days before the feud, they were a communal resource devoted to healing, a factory to produce medicines from herbs. Carved niches in the wall once held jars of healing remedies. Now they contained poisons.

We paused before a closed door. "They're inside, both of

them," she said. "He never buried her." I opened the door quietly, stepped into a fan-shaped room with alcoves in the opposite walls. A plain wooden coffin stood in one alcove. In the other, he lay on a bed, covered with blankets, even though the day was warm and the air inside the cave felt mild. He knew me immediately. The burly king of the caves lay still, and the great black mustache dominated his sallow face like an irrational patch of fur on the head of a wax doll. The eyes which had shot lightning looked cloudy and weak. "It's a quiet poison," he said, "slow but painless." This man tried to kill me, I thought, but he looked so helpless, I felt no anger.

"I can't play your fiddle, *mago*," he said. "It's too big." He turned his head, looked at the coffin. The viola case lay on the bench beside it. I rushed over, opened it, examined the Voice of Manush, sighed with relief. No sign of damage. "I'm alone," he said, "and my people have surrendered. Do me one last favor, *mago*, a small one. Keep me alive a little longer. Before I took the poison, I stepped outside, and Fedele—you know, the one they call king of the trulli—the bastard saw me and threw one. He missed, but the scummy bastard will lie and say he got me. If I die now, he'll brag he did it. Just a few more days, *mago*." I shook my head, and with The Destiny in my hand, left the room.

FINALE

I have put before you life and death.
—Deuteronomy 30:19

1

Before leaving Italy, I phoned the library, tried to locate Gerry. Eventually, I reached her at home. She spoke softly, "You saved my life, Harold. My doctor confirmed I did have cancer, but the surgery was not bad." She hesitated to say more, and I waited in silence. "And Harold, the whole thing gave new meaning to my life. I met someone on the staff of the hospital I now love very much, and we're together." I wondered who it was, male or female, this new light in Gerry's life. I hung up the phone with a feeling of relief, touched with sadness.

I carried the Voice and a backpack on a voyage to Istanbul. Wanting to see Ametra again, wanting to talk to her about our son, I flew to the island of Samos from Athens, walked the harbor of Samos town, straining my eyes to search over the horizon for Fluaria.

If you look at a large-scale chart of the Aegean northeast of Samos in a location I can point out to you, nothing is recorded there but a reef. I chartered a boat and got as close as possible, but saw only rocks. The Greek steering the boat was terrified we would smash up. "Nothing there but trouble, you damned fool," he shouted in exasperation, and we turned back.

The time was off season, so ferries were not running, but I found a rusty little Turkish ship bound for Kusadasi. The captain, an affable man, spoke some French, and I tried to describe the island of Fluaria. Halfway to the Turkish shore, we looked at a chart, and he pointed to the horizon, to a bank of clouds over an empty reef. I gave it up.

From Kusadasi, I went to Ephesus, walked out to the site of the temple of Artemis, one of the seven wonders of the ancient world. A family of Gypsies in a donkey cart saw me walking with the viola case in my hand. They waved at me, looked excited, put their heads together. I imagined—just imagined—they detected the Voice of Manush.

And why not? The Voice was alive, with powers beyond my comprehension. Perhaps it had already set forces in motion to steal the next player.

I saw nothing left of the temple but a solitary column. The Emperor Justinian, I knew, had robbed the columns for the Hagia Sophia, the wonder of Istanbul. I sniffed in vain for a scent of Artemis.

My job was to hand the Voice over to an agent of Death. What would happen to it? Perhaps nothing ever happened to the Voice against its will. Not an instrument, but a living force. If Death had the power to destroy it, wouldn't he have done so by now? After all, Stradivari and Mihaly made the Voice more than two hundred and fifty years ago!

I was in no hurry to reach Istanbul, took the bus to Izmir, looked out the window, watching for Gypsies. At the security checkpoint in the airport, they opened my viola case. The guard smiled and asked, "Topkapi Quartet?" I didn't know what he meant.

Behind me, a dark nervous passenger, wearing a hearing aid and carrying a large camera bag, spoke loudly in Italian, "*Ipersensibile pellicola.*" Supersensitive film. Seated in the lounge, he kept a pocket calculator in his hand, and I noticed a watch on each wrist. Peculiar. Against the wall, a portly man in uniform startled me—he had the figure of Russell Flambard.

My imagination went wild. The passenger was a terrorist, I imagined, one of the wristwatches a timing device, his little film canisters loaded with Semtex, and the pocket calculator contained a narrow tube which fired a detonating projectile. He evoked a vivid daydream:

I run to the chief of security, who speaks English, tell him I'm Major Bird from the United States, on a secret mission. He looks at me without speaking, no expression on his face. I continue, say I'm travelling in a false identity, and my work is so delicate I carry no papers to prove who I am. All I can tell you is the code word, Operation Destiny. He looks at me steadily with a hard, skeptical smile. Do you recognize the password? I ask. Perhaps, he replies. What do you want?

I want to alert you to a dangerous passenger who slipped through the security process. He's carrying explosives.

The security chief gathers his men and follows me to the lounge. The passenger, seeing us, points the calculator at the camera bag at his feet. I lunge at the bag, throw it across the room, as the Turkish security men close in. The man holds the calculator up to the ear with the hearing aid, and we hear a noise like a loud slap. It blows a hole through the left side of his head, and as blood flows out his nose, he falls on his left shoulder, his glasses tumbling to the floor. A portly figure in a Turkish uniform stands over him, and Russell says to me, "Thanks for your help."

All in my imagination, but the fantasy was a commentary on my working relationship with death. I would have saved the lives of people in the airport because the Leech had sent me there. He intended me to save them, because in the grand scheme of things they were not ready to die. Why did he reveal the game to me? Why not? I'm no Pesh. But I had assumed all along I was working against him. That was part of the game. My immortal playmate, the mortal presence I called the Leech, could he be a guardian of life as well as the angel of death? The answer to that one, Gypsies say, is in a song I never heard.

My plane landed in Istanbul, which felt like a city under military occupation, full of uniformed patrols, guards, military police with automatic weapons slung over their shoulders. When I stared at a sentry, he swung his carbine, pointed the barrel at me.

I stayed at the Konak Hotel, between the Hagia Sophia and

the Blue Mosque in Sultanahmet, the oldest quarter of the city. The manager of the Konak, a young man with a double chin and slick black hair, dressed in a pin-striped suit, glanced at my viola case and introduced himself as Bogdan Richter from Salzburg. "*Bratschenspieler?*" he asked. In English, I admitted I played the viola. "Professionally?" he insisted, switching to English.

"Retired," I said.

"You'll be interested in the couple seated by garden," he enthused, taking my elbow. "Nice folks. Viennese. Survivors of Topkapi Quartet, violin and cello. Charming ensemble, Topkapi, but they did fighting all the time, like French cats with German dogs, *immer zankung, immer zankung*, you know what I mean, perpetual war, *bis zur Vernichtung kämpfen*. Each year we did expecting them to fall apart. They surprised everybody, managed twelve seasons to stay together. Lucky for us, because not much chamber music is in Istanbul. Now these two going home, returning to Austria."

He instructed a man in a white coat and black tie to turn on the music, and soon I heard Mozart's last piano concerto coming out of speakers in the garden. Richter patted my shoulder. "Garden is word for *paradise*. You'll find it in Koran. And this hotel is as close to paradise as government will permit. Turkey is secular state, you know. But kitchen never closes, and staff enjoy duty round the clock. Let them know your desires."

"Lovely here," I offered.

"Is a fake palace," he replied.

"Who owns the Konak?" I asked.

"Touring Club of Turkey. For more than hundred years, Konak mansion was *verfallen*. Now is, how you say, *übertrieben*, excessive renewal. They exaggerated what means 'luxury hotel.' Double carpets, velvet curtains, elegant furniture, gold and marble fixtures. From a ruins they make a sultan's palace."

My room on the first floor was overwhelming, with a delicate pattern of wildflowers on the walls and two turkish carpets on the floor. Glass petals shaded the bulbs of bronze lamps shaped like rosebuds on the walls. A gold-framed oil painting showed the Golden Horn, reflected on the opposite wall by a mirror in a huge gold frame carved with birds and flowers. On the windows, velvet drapes covered thick lace curtains like hoop skirts on petticoats. The velvet easy chair in the corner displayed a heavy fringe on its bottom edge. Little statues of birds roosted, nested, or pecked on every marble surface. I left the Voice on the bed, on a huge mattress in an old-fashioned brass bedstead with oil lamps on marble tables guarding each corner. If they stole The Destiny now it would save me trouble, I thought. Who cares?

But I locked the door of the room and sat quietly in the garden, gazing out at the fountain, wondering how to approach the Viennese couple. The place felt elegant, quiet, peaceful, and the marble fountain diffused an alabaster mist. Attentive presences lined the edges, three Graces, nine Muses, marble witnesses to drama in the garden. The woman glanced at me out of the corner of her eye and smiled. She was laying out a deck of cards. Her husband, a large man, sat contemplating the fountain, palms on his thighs. His massive jowl, carved to look steady as a vise, was shaped to hold down a fiddle. The waiter, bringing me a glass of wine, whispered, "They continue."

"Continue what?" I asked.

He replied in Turkish. I thought he said *paradise*. Approaching their table, I noticed the Viennese woman was spreading a Marseilles tarot deck. She looked up at me, looked up from her cards, and said, "*Liebeskrank!*"

"Harold Child," I replied in English. "My name is Harold Child."

"But you are lovesick, Harold Child," she insisted.

"She enjoys mysterious," her husband offered gloomily, and pointed to a chair. "Sit down, *Herr* Child."

"Your card, my dear," she said, handing me Number Six of the Greater Trumps, the one called *The Lover*. "You look terrible, poor darling. Victim of *un grand passion*, and very sad. Losing the one you love."

I drew up the chair her husband had pointed out and sat down. "Best of all," he confessed, "I love the late quartets. Have you performed the Rasumovskys?" Even though Richter had failed to introduce us, he had not hesitated to talk about me. They knew I played the viola.

"What we need right now is trio music," she said.

"I do have something with me," I replied, "something I never played before."

She put the tarot cards away in their box. "Show us," she urged. "We need to play something." I hurried to my room, came back with parts for *Hermes in Egypt*.

"Attributed to Mozart," I said.

"Such things I never believe," he replied, reading through the score for violin.

"Not bad," she added, reading through the cello part. "For fake Mozart, not bad."

"Try it on your instruments," I suggested to them. "I need to take a walk."

2

Russell had instructed me to stay at the Konak because it was near the place he expected me to sell The Destiny. I wanted to look it over. Fourth shop from the corner, where the Divan Yolu begins, between a little hotel and a tourist agency. The place was shut. In the window I saw two violins, a banjo, a mandolin, and an accordian. A sign in English read, *Second-hand instruments. I buy, sell, and trade.*

I walked back down the main street, the Divan Yolu, to the park, right at the corner where the street begins, where a family of Gypsies camped, only about three hundred and fifty feet from the shop. If I want to believe in coincidence, I should not be a Manava. Destiny rules and death obeys, but music governs destiny.

The solitary police guard, a portly figure in military uniform, ignored the Gypsies. They had a fire going between two wagons, and they looked beautiful to me—sunburnt faces, long curly hair, sparkling eyes, white teeth. A skinny, little boy stood apart, facing a high stone wall, making echoes with a jew's harp, while a man, some distance away, standing with his back against a wagon and facing the fire, strummed a guitar.

Sneaking up on the kid, I picked him up in one arm, carried him to the other side of the wall. He didn't cry out, but stared at me with lively interest. Gypsies are expected to steal children, but who would want to kidnap a skinny little Gypsy? I spoke in Romany, put a silver coin into his hand. "Tell me, little nephew, what's your name?"

"Manava Gyorgy, Uncle," the boy replied.

"And what's the Manava family doing in the heart of the city?" I asked, pouring coins into his hand.

The boy shrugged. "Waiting for something," he said. I pulled a little notebook from my pocket, tore out a page, and with the book on my knee, slowly and carefully in Romany, wrote out full instructions. "I can read," the boy said. He leaned over my arm curiously and read out loud, "What's the only thing on earth that has one body and three voices?" He stepped away, threw back his hair and gazed at me, puzzled. "Everyone in the family knows that one. The answer is Manush." I smiled, nodded, continued writing. "What are you writing now?"

"A message to your father."

"Why? Go over to the wagon and talk to him!"

"He has holy work to do."

The boy looked at me suspiciously. "Whose work is it?"

I folded the sheet of paper. "It's the work of Manava Mihaly. Your father will understand." I ruffled the boy's wild black hair and handed him the note.

3

I returned to the Konak and dined with the Viennese couple. Since we were the only guests, we ate in the garden, under the faces of Muses and Graces. The cellist kept her score of *Hermes in Egypt* on the table in front of her. "We like your fake Mozart," she said. "I have some questions about the bowings."

Richter, standing behind us, said, "Clear night, no clouds, and the moon is full minus three. Garden is beautiful by moonlight."

"We need the moon," I agreed. About three o'clock in the morning, with the moon overhead, I showed up with The Destiny and the Hermes music. The waiter in the white coat whispered, "They in garden. Still waiting." Richter had arranged three music stands with candles, but the moonlight was bright enough. We rehearsed the piece five or six times, then performed—for Richter, for the waiter, for the marble faces of Muses and Graces. I played for Papio Tamás, Little Mamo, Ametra and my son; I even played for Russell. The music was indescribably beautiful and left me with a feeling of gratitude, profound gratitude my life had brought me to that moment. Inevitably, I was there. Inevitably, I would hand over the Voice. There was no need for me to play again. As if kissing the face of the instrument, I put my lips to the sound holes. Should I suck out the air? On the contrary, I blew into it, gave it my soul.

4

When I returned to Divan Yolu later in the day, the tiny shop was open. The man inside had a curious birthmark on the left side of his face which ran from under his eye across the cheek to the jaw. Not red or brown, but the color of ashes. And the tips of his fingers were smooth all around, without fingernails. He said, "Not much call for violas these days." Peering into the soundholes, he read the ticket. "Fake Stradivari. Not worth much. Too big to play under the chin." I took what he offered.

There was only one Gypsy wagon left in the park. I waited in the shadows across the street, stayed to witness the next step, waited till fire broke out in the wagon. Somewhere an alarm went off. People ran down the street to the park. The shopkeeper ran out with them, a bucket in his hand. From the other direction, two ragged figures appeared and dashed into the shop. One stood in the doorway until the other reappeared with a sack under his arm. Both ran up the street, away from the park.

I walked back to the Konak alone, wondering how I would live without The Destiny. Would Death take me, I wondered? If I insisted?

But the Leech had work for me to do. All over the world, mortals rush their mortality. They fling themselves at oblivion, striving to leave before their time, or try to kill people not destined to die. His heavy work is to keep them from dropping out too soon, to prevent premature deaths, to regulate the death rate, to serve as a guardian of life. We healers of the highest degree are his agents.

On my return to Greece I paused in Samos again, stood on the shore, straining to see a dark mist on the horizon that might be the clouds over Fluaria.

5

I want to tell you how The Destiny pursued me, but as a Gypsy storyteller out on the *puszta* would say as he sets aside his fiddle to gaze into the fire, it's an important story, and the hour is getting late. Let's save it. Next time you come to see me, I'll tell what happened, and we'll play some music.